A Bit About Vivian

. The Girlz and Me .

Rick Tyson

For my family, and of course, the soccer sisters.

PART ONE

CHAPTER ONE

BAD DAY, WEIRD YEAR

JUST SAW MY DAD CRY for the first time. He didn't know I was there, standing outside what was once his and Mom's bedroom. They were on the phone, arguing again.

"Come on, Grace. You said this would be okay."

I peeked around the door to see him sitting on the end of the bed, staring at the floor in front of him.

"I know, but…"

"Yes."

"No."

"I know it's not your fault. I get it, but can you at least try? We've had this reservation for two weeks, and the Smiths got a sitter and had to move things around to join us."

He rubbed his face with his free hand, trying to smooth out the lines of sadness around his eyes.

"No."

"No, I'm not, and don't try to turn this around on me. I'm not the one avoiding the other."

During a long silence, he looked up at the ceiling.

"Well, that's what it feels like lately. You always find reasons for us not to spend time together."

And that was when it happened. A tear rolled down the side of his face as he closed his eyes and shook his head ever so slightly. I felt like I got the wind knocked out of me.

Dad never cries. He's always laughing and totally embarrassing me in front of my friends. Seeing him look so sad and so alone makes me want to cry too.

But I don't have time to cry because suddenly Dad's voice changes into a low, angry whisper, which totally freaks me out.

"All right, Grace, whatever you say. But you call the Smiths. You tell them you need to work late again. I'm tired of doing all the explaining for you."

Dad hangs up and tosses the phone over his shoulder onto the bed before putting his face into his hands.

Something tells me that I can't stay here, that I'm not supposed to see this. So I tiptoe backward into my room and quietly shut the door, totally unsure of what to do. *Do I go back out there? Do I hide in here for a while, or do I—*

"Hey!"

I spin around to see my older brother James walking out of our closet trying and, oh no, nearly failing to wrap a towel around himself before retreating back behind the door.

"Jeez, Vivian. You have to remember to knock, you know?"

James and I have been sharing my bedroom since Mom and Dad started sleeping in separate rooms last summer, which is awful in every possible way. Like now, for example.

"Can you get out of here so I can go use the shower?"

First seeing Dad fall apart and now this. "Sorry. I'm sorry. I'm leaving."

I grab my hoodie lying on the end of my bed and make a run for it down the stairs and out to the porch, texting frantically the entire way.

> Me: *GirlZ! Anyone able to hang out? I'm walking to town. Now. I have to get out of my house. Serious face emoji. Running girl emoji. Candy emoji.*
>
> Mia: *Totally. See you in 10. Thumbs-up emoji.*
>
> Lucy: *I think so I just need to ask my mom.*
>
> Katie: *Yep. Heart emoji.*

Thank God. I don't know what I would do without my friends, especially in moments like this. I can't unsee the images of Dad being sad and James in a towel. I rub my eyes extra hard to try to squeeze out the mental images, but it doesn't work. Just another super-bad day in a super-weird year.

CHAPTER TWO

MY GIRLZ

CE-CREAM CONES COMBINED WITH THE never-ending comedy of being around my friends lightens the heavy weight I've been feeling since I slammed the front door of my house behind me. Everyone's engrossed in one of Mia's drama-filled stories about her older sister.

"And Emma has been totally FaceTiming with Crush Boy for, like, weeks. 'Blah, blah, oh, you're so cute, blah.' So they went out for a bike ride, just them, together after school yesterday, and then Emma said that she leaned in to *kiss* him." Mia pauses for effect.

"What?" everyone screams in unison.

"But right before the big smooch, he *burped* in her *face*! And here's the thing," Mia continues, all animated, trying to get her words out before her laughter overwhelms them, "Emma *still* kissed him anyway!"

Ew.

And that does it. An uncontrollable, almost-electric jolt of laughter explodes inside of me just as I attempt to force down a big creamy gulp. But it's no use. I make an embarrassing *blarp* sound, and ice cream flies out my nose—chunky mint chocolate chip mixed with snot and spit. I once had a similar experience with milk, which was gross enough, but chunky ice cream out the nose takes sinus pain to an entirely different level.

The thing is, I just can't stop laughing, and that's fine because I don't want to.

"Oh, Vivian, that is *so* gross!" Lucy laughs. "Are you okay?"

Well, at least she can say something. Mia and Katie are doubled over with their hands over their mouths, laughing so hard they can't even speak.

"Yes, I'm okay," I say through gulping laughter. "But really? A kiss *after* a burp to the face?"

Tears roll down my face, chasing the gross combination of snot, spit, and ice-cream chunks pouring over my mask, which is now more of a napkin than Covid protection, and oozing down onto my hoodie. But that's okay—the earlier events at home are far away now. I just wish my nose would stop hyper-tingling as I try to pull myself together. One thing is for sure—this is the part of the day I don't want to end.

Speaking of which, "Who wants to take another lap around town?"

Everyone kind of looks at me with *Huh?* expressions on their faces.

"For what?" Katie asks.

"I mean, we can get some gum at CVS," I offer, hoping someone will think that's a good idea. "And I really need some napkins."

"More like a bath," Mia says, which gets her a light punch on the arm as I make a pretend sad face.

"I don't have napkins, but I've got gum." Katie digs around in the front pocket of her jeans. "Oh, I know, why don't we go back to my house and play soccer in the backyard?"

It's as if a supersized bag of gummy worms just magically appeared in front of me. A boring run to CVS for gum is better than going home, but the offer of soccer in Katie's backyard is perfect, perfect, perfect. And all the GirlZ agree.

That reminds me… "Mia, what time do you want to start the cozy-couch movie tonight?"

Mia pops the last of her strawberry cone into her mouth and, through a chewy mouthful, says something that sounds like "Mom says we can FaceTime you after dinner. By the way, what happened today?"

"Oh." *Where do I begin?* "Well, my parents got in an argument on the phone, and my dad was… pretty upset."

Mia looks at me, waiting. I don't want to share that Dad was crying. The image is still too fresh, and I don't even know if I'm able to process it yet.

I go on. "And then, ugh, then I walked in on my brother in a towel!"

Mia's eyes go wide. "Wait, you were in just a towel?"

"No! He was! James. I walked into our bedroom without knocking just as he was going to go take a shower. Oh, it was so gross."

Mia laughs at that, then I say, "I hate not having a bedroom anymore. I mean, my *own* bedroom. I seriously need some me space—any me space. I don't have any-where to go to just be alone or paint or even FaceTime with you guys."

"Do you have an attic?" Lucy asks. "Maybe you can hang out up there if it's big enough." Lucy has been quiet on our walk until now, but that's an interesting idea.

I start to noodle it over. "We do," I say. "I never really go up there, but… that might be a good idea. Even a dusty old attic would be much better than having my smelly brother in my room."

Before I ponder this little plan any further, the four of us round the corner and walk up the driveway to Katie's house. As usual, a bag's worth of soccer balls is spread all over her backyard, some in the goal her dad built and others lying around, waiting for action.

Katie throws her blue-tinted blond hair into a high ponytail and, as only she can do, rips a shot into the upper corner of the goal. This is what Katie does—prac-tice, practice, and practice soccer in the backyard, rain or shine, snow or mud. It's why she's always our team's top goal scorer. My shot has some juice on it, too, as it makes that familiar rippling sound while rolling down the back of the net.

"Want me to shoot on you, Vivian?" Katie asks as she rounds up the balls to the center of the backyard.

"Sure!" I step between the posts.

Even with the muddy winter leftovers lying around the goal, there's no way I can get more gross than I already am, given the poor state of my ice-cream-snot-covered hoodie. But I need to have something warm to walk home in, so I toss it to the side. I'm down to just a tank top and sweats now.

Lucy, on the other hand, is all bundled up in her puffy white parka and wearing a beanie. "Jeez, V. Aren't you freezing like that?"

Lucy Gooding never even saw snow before this year because she just moved here from Florida last fall with her mom and her sister. She must think I'm crazy standing in fortysomething-degree weather in just a tank top and pants with mud and snow at my feet.

I guess Katie's mom is thinking the same thing, because she says, "Hi, girls! Oh, Vivian Hopewell! You're going to freeze like that, honey. Do you want one of Katie's sweatshirts?"

Katie fires a shot to my left, and I slide through the muddy corn-kernel-like snow to make the save.

"That's okay, Mrs. Adams. I'm good," I say, brushing the slush off my pants and arms.

"Well, you may think so, but I don't want you walking home soaking wet like that. I'll grab a sweatshirt for you."

Zoom. Katie must not have liked me saving that last shot, because she buries her next one in the upper-right corner.

Just as I move to catch Katie's next shot, Mia finally looks up from her phone. "My mom says we need to decide on the timing for tonight's movie. Oh, and we need to figure out what to watch."

Mia and I invented the "cozy-couch movie" concept when school got shut down during Covid last year. It's genius. First, we get on FaceTime to make popcorn "together" with our tablets propped up in the kitchen. Sometimes our moms help us bake things too.

Once the snacks are all ready and we're in our comfiest pajamas, each on our own couch, we count, "Three, two, one," and press Play to start the movie at exactly the same time. So it's sort of like we're in a movie theater together, even though we can't be.

"How about *Thor*?" I ask in response to Mia's question. I love Marvel movies and binge-watched every one of them this year on repeat.

"I'm tired of *Thor*," replies Mia. "Let's watch *Captain Marvel*."

"That's fine." I've seen *Captain Marvel* probably twenty times, but watching Carol Danvers save the world never gets old.

Oops! I'm thinking about movie-selection ideas, and I'm not ready when Katie almost knocks me off my feet with a shot that glances off my head.

"Sorry!" she yells. "Oh my God, are you okay?"

For such an absolute brute on the soccer field, Katie Adams is the nicest person I know in every other way. Her real name is Kate, but I think someone so sweet always has to have an *ie* at the end of her name. We've been best friends since preschool, along with Mia, and if it weren't for them, I don't know how I would have made it through this past year.

"I'm good. Nice shot, soccer sister," I say.

We smile at each other and do our little soccer fist-bump routine. Even with all the action in goal, the wet snow is giving me a chill, so I walk across the lawn to get the sweatshirt Katie's mom just brought out for me.

"Thank you, Mrs. Adams. I guess a dry hoodie is a good call."

"Of course, Vivian. Girls, it's getting close to dinner, and I need to get Katie here cleaned up and fed before she starts to work on her studies. But looking at you, honey, the cleaning part might take a while." Mrs. Adams grins.

Katie turns from the goal. "Mom, can I do the cozy-couch movie with Mia and Vivian too?"

"It's Sunday, honey. You know we need to work on your assignments for school."

That's true, and I feel kind of bad for Katie. She needs help with school and has a tutor in the afternoons. That usually means a lot of extra work and less time for fun. She spends Sundays after dinner in her room, working on tutor and school assignments—more work than the rest of the GirlZ usually have to do.

A big pickup truck pulls into the driveway, and Lucy's mom, Dr. G, waves and says that it's time for Lucy to go.

"My mom wants to have a family dinner with me and Lexi tonight," Lucy says as she walks toward the driveway. "Maybe FaceTime later!"

"Let's do a movie another night, Katie." I roll up my dirty sweatshirt. "You pick the movie."

Katie smiles and gives me a hug when her mom isn't looking. We GirlZ always hugged when we were allowed to before the distance rule thing, especially when we all really need one, like today.

CHAPTER THREE

HOME

A T LEAST BUSTER IS HAPPY to see me. He's been playing in the front yard and is even more filthy and muddy than I am, which is fine because dogs tend to get away with that more often than we kids do.

"Hey, Buster, buddy, buddy," I say in my puppy voice as I scratch his ears. "I'll bet you and I are the only ones who had fun playing outside today."

Buster whines at me and shakes his furry butt—puppy speak for "hurry up and play with me." That's fine because I don't want to go inside yet. I'm just not ready to deal.

"Want to play Olé?"

Buster stands on his hind legs, barks, and rests his front paws on me. He loves Olé, when I pretend I'm the matador and he's Ferdinand the Bull. I hold up my hoodie like a big cape as he jumps and twists in the air. His muddy paw prints add to its already-numerous layers of grime.

A breeze swirls around us, and a chill runs down my back. The temperature must be dropping. *All right, I'd better get inside.*

"Sorry, Buster." I sigh. "Fun's over."

I turn to walk toward the house. The sun is just slipping below the horizon. Clouds have come in, too, leaving a cold-looking grayish skyline practically swallowing my grayish house and brownish front yard. No rainbow colors here today. Trudging up the front steps, I look through the family room window. There's only one light on, and nobody seems to be in the kitchen. *Good.*

I tuck my hoodie under my arm and make a beeline through the kitchen and into the mudroom, where the laundry machine lives. Winter boots and jackets are cast about, neglected with… yes, mud on the floor, dried and crusty from today or even earlier in the week.

I quickly toss my gross hoodie and mask into the laundry before anyone sees me. A speed wash will keep Mom and Dad from giving me the usual lecture about getting my clothes all dirty.

Wait. It's the best cover story ever… No, Mom, that's not an ice-cream-snot-spit combo on my hoodie. It's just Buster's muddy paw prints. And I'm responsibly throwing it in the laundry before the stains set in.

It's the perfect crime.

I round the corner to the dimly lit family room to see Dad sitting in his favorite chair next to the fireplace. The single light I saw from outside is over his shoulder, reflected in the reading glasses perched on his shadowed face.

"Hi, Dad."

He doesn't say anything, and I notice he's holding a book open with one hand but not looking at it. His head is turned to the side, chin resting in his other hand, as he stares at something on the table next to him.

"Dad?"

"Oh. Hey, V." He looks up distractedly. "I'm sorry. I was kind of spacing out."

I walk over and offer a hug, which he returns with one arm. He pulls me onto his lap, and I notice a framed picture next to him on the side table. That must be what he was staring at.

"Is that the night you and Mom met?" I ask, reaching across him to pick up the photo. I already know the answer, having heard the magical story before.

"Yep. That's us. Long time ago." His eyes are fixed on the younger versions of him, Mom, and their friends. "Mom was working at that restaurant down in DC. I think I fell for her right there," he says quietly.

The photo was taken the summer when Dad had just finished serving in the Marines and Mom had just graduated college. Whoever took the picture at the end of the night snapped it right at the perfect moment when the new friends all broke into a laugh. Dad's eyes are still on the picture, and I can see the wheels turning in his brain. He's reliving the memory.

"Did you *kiss* her?" I ask loudly and giggle at the same time, bringing him back from his thoughts.

He laughs, rolls his eyes, and just says, "Girls…"

"Well? Did you?" I press, preferring funny Dad over moody Dad.

He looks up at me, all flustered. "I never got the chance. I mean, I don't think I imagined at the time that I could…" He nods. "But the next day, I wished I had, because I was sure that I would never see her again. And actually, I was almost right about that. It took a long time for me to, well, find her again, if that's what you call it."

He looks at me with his goofy Dad grin, and his eyes wander down to my arm. "Um, why are you wearing Katie's sweatshirt?"

What the heck? How does he…?

Oh, of course. It's Katie's soccer team hoodie with her number on the sleeve. Dad's our coach.

"We were practicing shots in her backyard, and my hoodie got wet, so Mrs. Adams let me borrow this one for the walk home."

"That's nice. Did you have fun with the girls today?"

"Yes, it was amazing. Um, where's Mom?"

Dad hesitates for a second before saying, "She's coming home from work soon. Had to finish up a few things there, I guess."

Dad and I look at each other for another second before I hand him back the picture. I want to hear the rest of the story about how he found Mom again, hoping it still has some happiness in it, but a voice in my head tells me not to. Not tonight, at least.

So I stand up, stretch, and look around the lonely room. The family room, as we call it, used to always have lights on throughout, giving it a bright, warm, welcoming atmosphere. That was when we would usually all sit together reading, talking, or just being. If we weren't sitting together, someone was at least passing through with a nod, a hello, or a kiss of greeting. Now it's this—one of us, one light, solitary.

Wait. So no one uses this room much anymore, except maybe Dad. *Hmm...* Perhaps it could be a new location for a fort—a temporary me place until I figure out a way to get my bedroom back. I could totally take over that corner near the half-empty bookshelf, maybe even build a walk-in...

Dad interrupts my thoughts. "Why don't you go on upstairs and take a shower, Little Miss Stinky Head? Please, before dinner. You're smelly."

I give him a little whack on the knee, with a dramatic "Hmph," and turn around to head upstairs.

I knock on my *own* bedroom door and walk in to see James lying there—on *my* beanbag, *no less*—in the corner of the room.

He looks up from his phone. "You have some black stuff on your chin."

I touch my face and look in the mirror, finding that my chin looks like I face-planted in a pile of chocolate mixed with glue. I have to smile as I think about the ice-cream fiasco one more time.

But look at me. The face in the mirror looks like a lost kid who just got spit out of a tornado. My brown hair is normally wavy, but right now it's damp and flat, and there's even a splash of mud on the right side of my face. I wrinkle my nose to make a funny face at my reflection and try to rub the goo off my chin.

"You look gross," James says, even though he's hardly looking up at me. Predictable.

"You *are* gross," I say back casually, not giving him the satisfaction of annoying me. "Pretty much all the time."

He does have a point, though. It's time for a much-needed soapy, hot shower. I grab my cow onesie and step across the hall to the bathroom.

When I walk back into my room, all squeaky-clean, I notice James has moved off my beanbag and back onto his bed. That's surprisingly nice of him. He's engrossed in some game on his phone. So I walk to the closet and dump the last of my dirty clothes into the hamper over-flowing with hoodies, towels, and T-shirts.

I might as well give it a try.

"Um, Mia and I are going to watch a movie tonight, and I'm making popcorn. Do you want some?"

James looks up like he only half heard me.

"Popcorn?" I offer again.

"Sure." He closes whatever app he's playing and gets off the bed. "Extra butter for me."

"As usual," I say over my shoulder as we make our way downstairs, my cow tail trailing behind me under my bathrobe.

James and I busy ourselves in the kitchen, getting the necessary popcorn-making ingredients together—tons of butter, of course, and as much salt as possible since Mom and Dad aren't here to make me stop pour-ing. I'm looking forward to watching an action-packed movie tonight with Mia. It will be a cherry on top of the rare perfect day outside with my friends. Plus, it's awe-some to be in a fresh, warm onesie with a fuzzy bathrobe before dinner—or anytime, for that matter.

I hear the front door open, and Mom comes in, still wearing scrubs from work and talking on her phone.

"Tell Dr. Andrews that I am the attending on call this weekend. I'll check on his patient tomorrow when I round." She pauses as she drops her purse and keys onto the hallway table. "Yes. I got it. Okay. See you tomorrow."

Mom puts her phone into a pocket, looks up, and smiles at James and me in the kitchen. "Hey, you guys."

"Hi, Mom."

Mom walks over to the sink to wash her hands. She rubs her eyes with a damp hand towel and takes a deep breath as she looks me up and down. "Um, ready for bed kind of early, aren't we?" It's a nice greeting, not the usual exhaustion typical of her busy days as a doctor at the hospital.

I lean into a hug. "I took a shower after playing soccer at Katie's house today and got into my cozy clothes."

As Mom eases into one of the barstools by the island, the questions begin about my day.

Yes, we walked to town...

Yes, we got ice cream...

Yes, it came flying out my nose...

"What?" she asks with a tired smile.

So I give Mom the whole story, and she laughs at my dramatic description of the ice-cream-nasal-projectile moment. I'm relieved that this little conversation with Mom is going well. She's happy that we GirlZ were together playing soccer at Katie's house. And I get extra brownie points for giving her more commentary than my usual one-word answers to her questions about my day. *Perfect. Everyone's happy.*

As she turns toward the kitchen counter, Mom notices our popcorn fixings. "I got a text from Mia's mom about your movie night. Have you had dinner yet? I think we have some pasta, then you guys can start the movie." Mom opens the refrigerator and starts pulling out the ingredients.

"I want to eat in my room tonight," James says.

Ugh. I cringe because I just know Mom won't say yes. He probably knows it, too, but that won't stop him. James has been doing this a lot lately—picking fights with Mom.

"Not tonight, James. We're going to eat together before the girls start the movie. Then you can hang out in your room."

This may not be the best time to remind everyone that it's actually *my* room, so I keep it to myself. Besides, I can already see where this is going—toward trouble, and James presses on to make sure it arrives.

"I don't feel like eating at the table. I'd rather just eat alone. I have homework to do."

Mom places her hand on the kitchen countertop, like she needs to balance herself or stop herself from throwing something. It's hard to tell which. I get the feeling this tension between them has been building up for a while.

"That's great, James. Just eat at the table, and then you can hang out all alone, all night. That's how this is going to work." Mom's eyes are set to glaring, not looking, and that means it's time to back off. It's a signal.

Of course, James chooses to ignore the signal and raises his voice. "I just want to have some private time to myself! Why is that such a big deal?"

"Listen, James—"

Wham! James slams his palm on the table with a slap that makes us all jump.

"Why won't you and Dad let me have my room back?" He points at me. "We don't like sharing a room together! It's not fair! I have to get dressed in the closet when Vivian's in there, and she totally walked in on me today! I'm tired of having nowhere to go to be alone, and she is too!" James is yelling now, rapid-fire anger meant to hurt.

Mom hasn't moved, and for some reason, I can't stop staring at her hand as she grips the edge of the table. I notice the strain across her knuckles, the stretched skin, and the pronounced veins. Perhaps squeezing the table so hard is how she keeps her voice so even when she says, "Well, James, just you wait. Maybe things will change sooner than you think."

That comment hangs in the air as Mom's eyes are still glaring right through him.

Huh? What does that *mean?*

But before I can ask, James says with sort of a snarl, "Yeah, whatever."

With that, Mom shifts her weight, and her expression changes. Her hand releases the table, almost like she's coming out of a trance. She isn't glaring anymore. Her tired eyes are now sad, too, with tears welling. She looks down to the floor, shakes her head, and walks out of the kitchen. I hear the front door open and close quietly.

James mutters something, turns, and disappears upstairs. I'm left standing in the kitchen, holding the popcorn bowl, all alone. All of us are now alone even though we are in the same house.

Of course, Dad heard everything. He quietly walks into the kitchen and puts an arm around my shoulders as I absentmindedly lean into him. He looks down at me for a moment then kisses me on the forehead.

"Give me a minute." He turns toward the front door leading to the porch, where Mom is sitting, looking out at whatever.

When fights like this started to be a regular occurrence last year, I would retreat to my bedroom, close the door, and crawl into my fort to read my books and pretend to be somewhere else. But I don't have the luxury of my own room anymore, and I feel trapped.

The box of boring pasta and jar of meat sauce still rest on the kitchen counter. My tummy is growling, but honestly, I don't even care about missing dinner tonight. Our dinners with Mom and Dad are usually quiet and awkward anyway. They always try to make conversation with us, but only us, not really with each other. It never feels real. So forget dinner.

My eyes wander to the family room and rest on that corner by the bookcase. As I take in the space, designs for a blanket fort fill my imagination. That's exactly what I need right now—a me place. A place to sit, sleep, read, and daydream, to get away from all this.

That's it. I'm going to make that corner mine.

I turn to head up the stairs, moving quietly so as not to draw the attention of Mom and Dad, who are still sitting on the outside porch. No need to get in the middle of that. I open my bedroom door.

"Don't bother me," James says, lying on his bed. "I want to be alone."

"Me too. This will only take a sec."

This has to be a one-trip effort because I don't want to be around James more than I have to. I grab a bedsheet from the closet that serves as the canopy I drape over my fort. I spread it down on the floor and pile on the necessary building materials—my favorite stuffed animals, two pillows, a blanket, books, a sketchbook, pens, markers, and my bag of emergency candy that I keep hidden under my bed. Oh, and there's my *special tech accessory* in my closet, which I tuck in there, too, before James can see me take it.

I fold the four corners of my now-portable fort over one another, take one more look around what was once my room, and tiptoe downstairs. I pause at the landing to see that Dad is still out on the porch, but Mom is not. She's probably out on a lonely walk.

I stand still, listening. Nothing. It's still quiet but less sad. My own feelings of loneliness are replaced with something else, a sort of calm. The prospect of building my own personal space is liberating. Let everyone else skulk around in front of each other while I tune them out in my cozy cave of blanketed comfort. And that's when it hits me—a plan. An Amazing Plan. This fort is going to be the way I get my room back!

My fort is going to be big. Really, really big! It's not just a place I get to escape to. It's going to be a nuisance for everyone else. I'll take over the entire family room, just for me. I don't care if my stuff gets in people's way. Let them trip over my pillows and my books. Let it be hard for them to find a place to sit and watch TV. That's the genius of my Amazing Plan. I'm going to just be in everyone's way until they can't take it anymore and realize they have to give me my room back. Until that happens, I can have a private place to hang out with all my stuff.

I can see it happening like this…

Mom and Dad, in annoying grown-up voices: "Vivian! Please get your stuff out of the family room! We keep tripping over your books and stuffed animals every time we walk in there!"

James: "Vivian! Where's the remote? Stop leaving it in your stupid fort!"

Me: "Oh, I'm sorry, parental unit and annoyingest brother in the world. My stuff is in your way? Okay. Well then, give me *my* room back!"

It's genius. I'm going to annoy my way back into having a room of my own.

And that's exactly what I set out to do. The bookshelf in the corner allows for a taller canopy than what I had in my bedroom, giving my fort a high ceiling and a more open feel. I always use a blue bedsheet as my canopy to create a dark sky. Then I lay out my books, sketchpad, and pencils in a corner with extra pillows so I can be propped up to draw. The pillows also act as camouflage for my emergency bag of candy, buried deep

22

so James doesn't find it. My puffy comforter stretches from end to end with more pillows, stuffed animals, and my Squishmallows in the corner. Finally, I plug in my special tech accessory—a starry-night mini projector that streams the universe across my canopy. The constellations are swirling all around me.

I crawl out of the fort to examine the family room, now noticeably smaller and harder to walk around in. *Perfect.*

I run into the kitchen and grab the popcorn, all for me. As I lie back in my fort, snacking on popcorn and admiring my handiwork, I begin to feel better. Now I have a me place. Thoughts of my amazing day with the GirlZ replace the sadness left by the painful events of the evening. My bunnies and puppies are in here with me, all of us lying back together on pillows and blankets.

Oh, and the best part—the TV remote is in here too. I brilliantly allowed enough sheet for the door part of my canopy to be able to fold up, providing a perfect view of the TV. Now the remote will live in my fort, buried, so it's a hassle for all who dare to try watching TV in the family room.

I'm all set, just in time for cozy-couch movie night with Mia. Maybe I'll rename it "cozy-fort movie night." I FaceTime Mia and give her a tour of my new fort in all its splendor.

"Wow!" she says, marveling at my innovation. "That's amazing!"

"Yes, it is." I turn on Disney+ and search for *Captain Marvel.* It's time to watch humanity get saved by a healthy dose of girl power. "And now I *own* the family room! Nobody is going to bug me tonight. That's for sure. Ready?"

"Ready!" Mia says.

"Three, two, one… go!"

CHAPTER FOUR

SOCCER SISTERS

"**R**EADY TO GO, HONEY?"

Coach Dad is in a hurry to get to the soccer field. It's our first game in almost a year. Finally.

"Yup," I say back as I stuff my bag with my goalie gloves and Katie's team hoodie.

"Ready."

As we roll out of our driveway, Dad tosses around some lineup ideas. "I think we should start Katie at striker and then move her back if we need to. What about Melissa? Should we start her at center fullback again this season?"

"Uh-huh." I look out the window, happy to think about nothing but soccer today. Dad always seems happy around us girls on the field too. He's sort of embarrassing when he gets overexcited, but he does make us laugh a lot.

The parking lot is packed. Cars, kids, and parents are coming and going as the fields turn over from one game to the next every hour. Everyone has their masks on. It's one of the many rules we have to follow to be able to play, but there are a lot of smiles underneath. We are back outside, playing soccer again. It feels almost normal. Whoever thought we would crave something as simple and boring as *normal*?

"Hi, V!" Katie sees me dropping my gear on the sideline and jogs over to me with the ball at her feet.

"Hi, Katie! Here's your hoodie."

It's just chilly enough this morning to wear an extra layer, but Katie never seems to notice the weather. She throws the sweatshirt on top of her bag, and we run out to the field. Dad asks her and Melissa to get the team together and run the warm-up drills while he warms me up in goal.

Most girls like playing in the field because they get to shoot and score. I started playing goalie last year. Nobody else wanted to do it, so I thought, *What the heck, why not?* I ended up being pretty good at it, and I really like making the big save, so I let Coach Dad know that I wanted to practice more.

He warms me up first, then the team makes an arc around the goal to work on shooting. The girls are all amped up with the usual pregame energy mixed with the giddiness of being together again on the field.

"Hey, sweet Mel!" I say as we greet with a fist bump. Melissa goes to the other middle school in our town, so I mostly get to see her during spring and fall soccer.

"What's up, Viv, girl?"

"Ladies, bring it in!" Coach Dad shouts. *Uh-oh, dorky-pregame-speech-time.* "Listen up. Listen up."

It's hard for us girls to stop messing around with each other—we have too much energy. Melissa whacks me on the arm, and I elbow her back.

"Girls!" Dad shouts, using his growly coach voice, which means he's serious now. He announces the lineup and goes through a few reminders about what to do when we have the ball and when we don't.

Katie pulls us all in together with an extra-loud "One, two, three—team!" Then we run onto the field to take our positions.

The other team is already lined up, and they look pretty amped up too. Their striker is doing a little dance over the ball in the center of the field and hyping up the girls around her. The referee blows her whistle, and it's on.

Our silliness quickly switches to intensity as Katie charges the other team's midfielder, steals the ball, and rips off a shot that sails just wide of the post. She sends a message: we're here to play. The other team has brought its own intensity, and I have a busy first half, with two diving saves and a breakaway shot that just barely gets by me.

Right before halftime, their center defender tackles Katie in the box, trying to stop her from getting off a clean shot. Katie goes down in a heap, grabbing her ankle.

"Hey! What the—" Melissa shouts from the center line, but the referee saw the foul and awards Katie a penalty kick.

She buries her shot in the upper corner, and we end up tied one to one at halftime.

The score stays that way well into the second half with lots of back-and-forth action and scoring chances for both teams. One girl takes a shot, and I just barely get my fingertips on the ball enough to knock it over the crossbar, leaving their team with a corner kick. Their center defender, the same one who tackled Katie in the first half, moves up to our end of the field and stands right in front of me. She's super tall and is trying to block my view of the field. As I move to step in front of her, she pulls on the back of my uniform when the ref isn't looking, just to annoy me.

Melissa sees what's going on and plants herself between the other girl and me as they start to jostle for position. It's like they are wrestling standing up, with elbows and arms pushing and shoving.

Melissa is getting annoyed, which often leads to her hot temper coming out. The other girl jumps backward and crashes into me, knocking me onto the turf, and that does it. Melissa spins around and pushes the girl with both hands. Then she stands over her, glaring. Melissa leans in close to the other girl, her finger pointed an inch from the girl's nose, and says something that sounds like a snarl before all the other players close in on the pair to try to break them up.

"Mel! You get out of there right *now*!" Dad yells loudly enough to let us know he means it as he steps on to the field.

The referee stops the game and jumps into the fray, pulling Melissa away from the other player, who is still lying on the ground. The ref takes both girls to the side of the goal and warns them to cut it out. Melissa tries to say something in her defense, but the ref puts her hand up as if to say, *just stop*. The girls nod at each other and kind of awkwardly fist-bump before walking back to their positions.

The break in play settled things down a bit, but the action picks right back up again at the whistle. Melissa steps in front of me and clears the corner kick out of the box to the center of the field. The other team takes control of the ball, and the rush is on as they pass the ball across the field in and around my teammates, who are caught off guard by the speed of the attack. The other team's forward breaks free, rushing at me all alone. I come out of the goal to try to make the save, but her shot flies out of reach and into the back of the goal.

The other team sprints to their shooter, and they mob one another in a big pile. The referee waves her arms, saying the game is over. They scored in the very last second to win, two to one. We're stuck in our tracks for a split second, with looks of disbelief on our faces as the sting of the loss settles in.

I can't believe it. I was so close to the ball. I put my hands over my head, feeling just so disappointed. But before I know what's happening, Katie, Mel, and all the girls rally around me with high fives and hugs.

Katie says, "You got us this far, V. You played great. It could have been five to one if you hadn't made so many saves."

Melissa leans into me with a hug as we walk back toward the bench. Coach Dad is calling us all in for a post-game wrap-up before we head home.

Something occurs to me, and I whisper to Mel, "What the heck were you saying to that girl you knocked to the ground? You looked like you were going to punch her in the face." I laugh at the memory, the craziness of it all.

Melissa laughs and says, "I said, 'You better stay away from my keeper, or I'll—'"

"Girls! Let's go! Come on in and take a knee," Dad yells, interrupting our little talk.

Melissa and I are the last to arrive at the bench. All the girls are in a semicircle around Dad, some sipping water bottles. All of us are sweaty and tired. Most of the team look pretty mad about the loss, but Dad keeps things positive.

"I'm so proud of you girls. That is a really good team over there, and you played them even. Frankly, it could have gone either way. We have some things to work on this week in practice, so come ready to play. Most importantly, take a quick second, look around at each other."

Awkward!

We don't really know what to make of that, so we drama it up with fake introductions mixed with laughter, which even gets Dad to laugh a little before saying, "Okay, girls, okay. The point is—here we are. Outside, playing sports again, together. How's that feel?"

No one says anything for a second, then Katie, in classic fashion, shouts, "Amazing!"

All the girls laugh and nod. Dad's a dork, but he's right.

Most of the girls have already grabbed their things and are walking toward the parking lot with parents and friends. The usual begging and pleading for a stop at the nearby ice-cream truck hits a high pitch of desperation, met with eyerolls by the parents as they dig around their pockets for money.

"Mel, stick around for a second," Coach Dad says. "We need to talk."

Mel puts her bag back down by the bench, looks at me with a little smile, and whispers, "Busted."

"Dad, come on," I protest. "Can we go get ice cream?"

He's looking at Melissa and holds a hand up at me, meaning I need to zip it.

I roll my eyes and pretend to dig around in my bag for something, but really, I'm straining to hear what he wants with Mel.

Dad leans down to look at Mel at eye level and says, "You need to keep that temper of yours in check, Mel. I don't put up with fighting of any kind on this team. Do you understand?"

Mel nods. "Yes, Coach."

"Besides," Dad goes on, "you are of no help to us if you get a red card and are thrown out of the game."

"Yes, Coach." Mel looks down for a second then up to meet Dad's eyes. "But I don't let anyone mess with my soccer sisters."

I look up at that and smile before pleading, "Dad! Can we *pleeeease* get ice cream?"

Dad says something else to Mel, and they both smile before she turns to get her stuff. Her mom is waiting for her by the parking lot and waves her to hurry up.

"All good?" I ask.

Mel smiles and nods. "All good, V. See you next week!" She shoulders her backpack and takes off running toward her mom with another wave.

Dad finally collects the cones, balls, and other stuff that goes into the big team bag that he lugs over his shoulder.

"Someone say ice cream?" he asks with a smile.

Finally!

We get our usual—SpongeBob bar for me and Bomb Pop for Dad—then walk toward the car. After he loads all our stuff into the trunk, he turns to look at me. "Nice game, V. You looked good out there."

"Thanks, Dad."

We lean against the car as we enjoy our treats and relive some of the game. He's only halfway through his Bomb Pop when, out of nowhere, he says, "I'm sorry about what happened in the kitchen last night with Mom and James—"

"It's not your fault," I say quickly, hoping not to get into this now.

"I know, V, but I also know that things aren't… well, easy at home these days. Haven't been for a while, actually. Are you doing okay? Is there anything you want to talk about?"

Ugh. I know why he's asking. He's being a dad. I'm already shaking my head before he finishes speaking.

"I don't feel like talking about all that," I say as I look down at my feet. "I just want to think about soccer today."

Dad is still looking at me, and a shadow of disappointment passes over his face. Then he nods like he gets it.

"Of course. I just want you to be happy, V, and if soccer makes you happy"—Dad leans in to hug me—"then we've got a long, fun season to look forward to. You better rest up, because I'm going to rip shots by you in practice this week."

"You wish!" I say back in my pretend-huffy voice.

We enjoy the remains of our treats, just the two of us together. We don't say another word about what happened the other night. We don't need to. Soccer fixes everything.

CHAPTER FIVE

EMERGENCY APB

"Hey, V?"

"Hmmmpff..."

"Vivian?"

I'm quietly pretending I don't hear my dad as I continue to add hints of bright color to my current masterpiece, a painting of a beautiful girl with flowers in her hair. Pink peonies, white lilies, and sunflowers each contrast vibrantly against the—

"Vivian!"

"Jeez! What, Dad?"

"*Please* take Buster for a walk! Come on. Why do I have to ask you *three* times?"

"Because I'm tired. I don't want to take Buster out."

"Well, I need you to. I'm trying to cook dinner, and he hasn't been out all afternoon. Can you please help me out?"

"I'm painting."

"And I'm cooking. So if you want dinner, come down from your room, and take Buster out—now!"

"Okay!"

Dad is always around now because he had to start working from home, making a lot of noise on his Zoom calls. So he always asks me—no, *tells* me—to do stuff. It's so annoying when he wrecks my me time.

Dad's little intrusion calls for a GirlZ emergency APB—Annoying Parent Bulletin. I hop on my iPad to see who can join me for a walk with Buster.

> **Me:** *GirlZ! This is an APB. Dad's being annoying. He wants me to walk Buster before dinner. Please help. Can anyone join me? Angry face emoji.*
>
> **Katie:** *I'd love to, but Mom is asking me to clean my room and set the table. APB here too!!! Sad face emoji.*
>
> **Lucy:** *I would love to, but I'm covered in paint and want to finish this project I'm working on. Sorry!! Heart emoji. Paint emoji.*
>
> **Mia:** *Absolutely! I'll meet you up at the pond?? Sparkle heart emoji. Rainbow emoji*
>
> **Me:** *Thanks GirlZ! Mia, see you there in ten minutes!! Clap emoji. Happy face emoji. Unicorn emoji. Heart emoji.*

Well, that's good news at least. Mia's always up for something. I'll bet she doesn't even ask permission and just walks out the door. I jump out of bed and throw on my hoodie.

As I get downstairs and put Buster on his leash, Dad leans around the corner. "Thanks."

"Sure…"

"And, V…"

"Yes?"

"Don't forget the poop bags."

Grrr… APB. APB. APB… Poop emoji x 100.

Okay, fine. Taking Buster out is always fun once we get out of the house. He jumps around and grabs the leash with his teeth like he wants to walk *me* somewhere, so I decide to just let him. Just a dog walking his human. We live near a pond, which is surrounded by woods and really pretty. There are a lot of trails to walk on, and Buster loves it. Not surprisingly, he's pulling me in that direction.

Mia is already waiting for me, wearing a white hoodie and these fancy jeans her mom gave her for her birthday this year. I think she even did her hair.

I smile at her. "You look all fancy."

Mia does a little half twist. "I needed to get out of my boring gray leggings that I've been wearing all day. I hardly ever get to wear real clothes anymore, sitting around at home."

I give her a hug, and we walk toward the trailhead. "I'm so glad you're able to help me walk Buster. Dad was getting grumpy, and me ignoring him made it worse."

"Funny how that happens," she says with a smile. "Here, I have extra." Mia hands me a piece of gum from her pocket.

We follow the trail into the woods that leads to the pond. It twists and turns. Leafy branches and brush neatly trimmed on either side create a maze-like feel. I love this pond, especially late in the day before dinner, because the sky is so pretty. The birds always make a lot of noise as dusk approaches, and it drowns out my thoughts. I'm still annoyed at Dad but less than before.

"I needed to get out of the house too," Mia says. "Emma was being all loud and dramatic talking with her friends on her phone. She always talks on speaker, even though Mom and Dad gave her earbuds for her birthday. It's always about this boy or that boy and the teacher they don't like… It's just endless."

I smile on the inside as she describes her older sister because that sounds just like Mia too.

"Hey, whatever happened to that boy who burped in Emma's face?" I ask through a giggle.

"Oh, you mean 'Burp Boy'?" Mia laughs, doing air quotes. "Emma is still crushing on him and gets mad at Mom and Dad when they finally tell her to get off the phone after FaceTiming with him for, like, hours every single night."

None of us GirlZ have any crushes on anyone at the moment. I mean, boys are as annoying as… well, the most annoying things on earth, I guess. But I know for sure that Mia is going to be the most boy crazy out of all of us. She's already in love with Tom Holland and watches *Spider-Man* at least weekly.

"Hold on a sec." I bend down to let Buster run off leash.

"I thought you weren't supposed to let dogs off leash up here." Mia blows a big pink bubble.

"I know, but who cares? He needs some exercise, and I don't see anyone who would be bothered by it. We have the trail all to ourselves. Go ahead, Buster—have fun."

Off he goes, running—actually, more like hopping— right alongside the water like he's chasing a fish, which can't be possible. Mia makes her silly snort laugh, and that makes me laugh too. I've moved on from my little outburst with Dad. It was a good idea to get out of the house so things didn't get worse and I didn't find myself getting into trouble. It's funny how dogs and friends are like medicine for parental-induced grumpiness.

Buster is running at full speed now, and he looks tempted to jump into the pond. I'm beginning to wonder about the consequences of muddy dog prints in the house. It turns out that would be the least of my problems, because all of a sudden, Buster freezes in place and turns his head toward something that made a noise in the woods. I don't know what he can see down the trail, but in a split second, he's gone, running full speed away from us.

Oh no. "Buster! Buster!" I yell.

Mia and I look at each other and turn to run after him—I think. I'm not even sure which way he went around a bend in the trail.

After a minute or two hurrying down a narrow, windy path that I never even knew was here, I stop. "Wait. Stay still."

Mia and I listen for puppy noises—barking or running paws. But the woods have gone quiet. It's like Buster found a secret door and just disappeared. I can only hear the two of us breathing heavily from running. *In fact, where the heck are we?*

As if she's had the same thought, Mia asks, "Where do you guys walk when you're up here?"

That's a good question.

"Usually, we just go around the pond. Buster has never run off like this before. Actually, we never let him off leash." My face starts to feel hot as I realize this is all my fault.

Mia looks at the path up ahead. "Where does that go?"

"No clue. We never come this way."

We start to run in that direction, only guessing where Buster might have gone. Not exactly the best plan. The stress of what Dad will say if I lose Buster overwhelms me. Buster is our family dog, but he's my pet. I always promised I would take care of him.

As this thought churns and storms in all directions around my mind, desperation begins to grow within me, and I imagine Dad's voice on repeat—*"Buster was your responsibility!"* over and over again, louder each time.

Dad really doesn't need another reason to be upset these days. None of us do. I can feel myself breathing harder, and a bubble of pressure is growing in my chest. Maybe Buster ran so far away that he got lost. *What if he's hurt somewhere?*

Tears begin to fall. "Mia…"

"It will be okay, V. Buster!" She keeps on calling his name.

I don't know what's worse—being scared that Buster is lost or hurt or being worried that Dad will be mad at me. That would mean more arguing in our house, more tears, and doors slamming… all because of me. Right now, I'm both scared and worried, which together lead to something worse: panic.

Panic makes bad decisions happen, like going way too far into the woods. That's exactly what we've done. Nothing here looks familiar. The trail is more overgrown than not. Now we're lost.

"We need to go back, Mia."

She looks at me as if she doesn't know what to do either, then we start to run back the way we came. Mom and Dad always tell me never to walk in the woods after dark, and here I am, breaking that rule too.

When I was little, Mom used to tell me that part of the reason I would feel upset was that my head was full of bad thoughts, and it was my job to chase them away. If I ran into Mom and Dad's room with a bad dream, she would hold me tight. "Close your eyes and be still," she would say. "Now, breathe. Just breathe." After I settled down, she would say, "Now chase those bad thoughts away. There's no room for them in your little head."

I would picture the bad thoughts as if they were a dark fog in my mind. Thoughts of pretty, bright colors would chase away the darkness. Green fields, blue skies, and the color of beach sand would calm me down, and my breathing would slow. I would feel more in control. Maybe that's why I like to paint pretty colors, land-scapes, and flowers.

So I stop running, stand still, and close my eyes. *Stop. Breathe. Clear my head.* I let the colors come into my mind and begin to breathe more slowly.

Mia is standing next to me now, just being there for me, not saying anything.

Stop. Breathe. Clear my head. Breathe in and out. Get control.

I'm beginning to feel better, just a little. I open my eyes again. The woods are quiet, but while that bothered me a few minutes ago, I feel it calming me now, and I start to think differently. Where would Buster go if he was done chasing a squirrel or whatever? Well, he would probably go home or maybe back to the pond to find me.

My eyes have adjusted to the fading light in the woods, so I can better see the outlines of the path against the leaves and brush.

I look at Mia. "Thanks. I sometimes need to slow things down in my head to think more clearly."

Mia smiles at me. "Someday, you have to teach me that one."

"You don't think that's weird?" I ask.

"No. I think we could all do better with tricks like that."

We continue walking, and I notice things that are familiar. The birch tree that Dad takes pictures of when it snows. Mom's rock, where she likes to bring us for picnics in the summer. We aren't far from the pond.

I hear a noise behind us. Footsteps on the path.

"You there," a man says not very nicely. He looks older than Dad and is coming toward us, leaning on a cane, walking with a noticeable limp.

"Who's that?" whispers Mia. I don't know him, and he certainly doesn't look very friendly. We take a step backward. This man is really big and wearing a long, heavy jacket. That cane looks like it might hurt, too, and I don't take my eyes off it.

As the man gets closer to us, he pulls his mask up over his face. His eyes stay on me the entire time, not blinking. *Stranger danger* flashes through my mind. Here we are, alone in the woods. It's getting close to dark, and this guy's got a mask on. As I look at Mia, I think about running. Her eyes tell me she's thinking the same thing.

The man looks at me for a long moment and stops. His breathing is heavy, but he manages to ask, "Did you lose your dog?"

Huh?

My feet are stuck in their tracks. Did I just hear that right? The man looks at me like he's waiting for an answer.

"Judging by that leash in your hand with no dog at the end of it, I'm guessing you did." He turns around and yells, "Honey! Over here," then looks at us again. "Your dog ran into my backyard and was barking at my cat, Whiskers, who likes to sit in the window. Caused a big fuss and made all sorts of a racket. Bothered all the neighbors too."

Just as I open my mouth to try to say something, I hear a voice behind him.

"Oh, Sam, just stop." An older lady—fortunately with a kind face—walks up with Buster, who's prancing alongside on the leash she's holding.

"Buster!"

The lady drops the leash, and Buster runs right over to us. He's all excited, paws up on my shoulders, licking my face and doing the same to Mia. He's not hurt—or bothered by anything, for that matter. Just a happy dog who's been running around free in the woods. I can't believe it, and a wave of relief washes over me.

"Yup, I guess he's yours," says the lady.

"Thank you so much," I say, trying to calm Buster down and hug him at the same time. "I'm really sorry if he caused any trouble."

The man with the cane starts to say something, and the nice lady takes hold of his arm. "Not too much trouble," she says, smiling. "We have a leash hanging in our garage, and after we gave your dog a treat, he was a very good boy. My name is Louise, and this is Sam. We live at the end of the path in the gray house. I've seen you walking your dog—Buster, is it?—around the pond before, so I guessed he had run off on you."

I put Buster back on our leash and hand the other one back to Louise. "I hope your cat is okay."

Sam looks at me, and his firm gaze has softened into amused appraisal. "He's fine, young lady. Just keep that dog on leash next time. You girls have to get home before it gets too dark. Do you know your way?"

"Yes. Thank you," I say, a little embarrassed.

We head toward the pond with Buster to get back on the road to my house. We're moving quickly, more like running, because I know Dad is wondering where I went. I'll probably get in trouble for being late to dinner, but I'm fine with that. Things could have been much worse.

Mia stops and looks at me. "Are you okay, Vivian?"

"Yes, I am now."

Buster rests his front paws on my chest, looking for an ear scratch.

"I just… I didn't want to lose Buster, and I can't imagine the trouble it would have caused at home. We have enough going on at the moment."

Mia smiles. "I had it under control. I was going to say it was all my fault. That I'm the one who let Buster off leash, and then he ran off. I wouldn't let anything bad ever happen to you."

Mia has this very matter-of-fact expression on her face, like she's thinking, *Of course that was what I was going to do. Why not?* That's my Mia. Social butterfly, yes. A little flaky at times, yes. But always there for me? Also, yes.

Without a word, she hands me another piece of gum and continues walking. I follow in her footsteps, feeling immensely grateful for a friend like Mia at times like this.

Oh no, more tears… dang it.

We take a turn in the trail that leads to the main road, leaving the pond and this whole silly adventure behind us. The sun is down now, and the evening light is almost out. A bouncing flashlight is approaching from up ahead with James on the other side of it.

"Hey, V. Dad wants you home for dinner. He made his lasagna again."

Mia and I look at each other. She smiles and winks at me then turns to walk toward her house.

"Do you want us to walk with you?" I ask. "It's dark."

"Nope. All good. I know what I'm doing." And she waves over her shoulder with her back to us while walking down the street.

James gives me a little nudge with his shoulder as he walks by me. "Come on, Vivian. Let's go."

"Yes, let's."

What a night. I'm exhausted.

Buster, of course, had the time of his life, terrorizing squirrels, a cat… and me. We walk into the house together, with Buster leading the charge, shaking his butt and trying to hop on Dad.

"Hi, Dad."

"Hey, V," he says over his shoulder. He pulls the lasagna out of the oven and examines it. "Dinner is almost ready. Where were you guys?"

"We went up to the pond and around the trail."

"See any fish?" he asks, with one of his lame dad jokes.

I help set the table and pour the water. As we all sit down, Buster curls up and falls asleep by my feet, snoring, tired out from our secret adventure.

CHAPTER SIX

THE RELOCATION PLAN

"JAMES, WILL YOU HELP ME set the table?" Dad asks.

I can hear the kitchen hustle-bustle from the comfy confines of my fort in the next room. Mom's cooking, and Dad's futzing with whatever.

"James? God, that kid," he says under his breath.

"Just walk up and get him, Jim," Mom says, sounding a little huffy.

Dad seems to ignore her—always a big mistake—and yells, "James! Get down here, please!"

"I'm coming! Jeez!"

Another nice night with the fam around the dinner table. Yay...

I have expanded the square footage of my fort over the past few weeks by building out a corner for a larger drawing space. My fully extended sleeping bag is at the center of it all. I could probably park my bike in here.

"Vivian?" It's Mom.

Time to one-up big brother... "Yes, dear parent?"

I can almost feel the telepathic power of Mom rolling her eyes.

"Get washed up for dinner, please, and pour the water and milk for the table."

I do as I'm told, and we settle into the usual not-so-comfortable dinner vibe. This one, for some reason, feels extra strained. Mom and Dad aren't even pretending to talk to James and me like they usually do. I'm not sure what's up, but the sounds of clinks and clanks of forks on plates climb up the walls and hang over us.

The best plan of action under these circumstances is to eat as fast as possible and get the heck out of here. So I snarf down my spaghetti and, after clearing my plate, head up to my bedroom to take control of the beanbag. I deliciously overhear James asking where the remote to the TV in the family room went. That should keep him busy for a while. I miss having my beanbag to myself. I think I should sneak it down to my fort.

Or should I?

My eyes drift up to the ceiling. *Hmmm. The attic…*

I take a peek outside my bedroom door to make sure the coast is clear and tiptoe past the bathroom and down to the end of the hall, where an old creaky door opens to a narrow staircase. Everyone is still downstairs, so now is my chance.

The light switch by the door illuminates the old wooden stairs, which curve around the interior frame of the house. I reach the top step and take in the view of the shadowy lumps and shapes along the dark floor that stretches from one end of the house to the other. I pull a string to turn on a single bulb overhead, and light spreads across the room that I know nothing about but has always been here, just above my bedroom. The air around me feels still and unsure, as if the space doesn't know what to make of my intrusion. I gently step from end to end, stopping to visit various piles of memories—the old chairs we would use when company came over, my first dollhouse, some of James's old baseball bats, and an entire corner dedicated to the boxes that hold Christmas ornaments and decorations carefully stored from year to year.

The locks of the window on the end wall are turned inward, sealing the space against the outside air. I look over my shoulder, as if someone might be watching, and try to open it, but it's shut tight. I bang it with my hand, and that does the trick. Cool night air comes rushing through, instantly refreshing the old air that was trapped up here for who knows how long.

I turn to survey the entire space. A low mattress and bedside table could fit next to the window, leaving plenty of space for a desk. My beanbag can sit on the opposite wall. With a good cleaning and a few desk lamps, this place would be cozy. I can see this idea working out, building my own bedroom for guaranteed privacy.

But then another plan begins to form in my mind. At first, it's just a little flash of an idea, but as it continues to evolve, it becomes more and more genius. Why should I upend myself from my own bedroom? I've basically already done that with my fort. No, there can be another way, something no one will see coming. I'm going to transform this space into the room that James absolutely, positively has to have.

That's it! I'm going to get *my* room back.

I look around and take stock of the attic through a new perspective. What kind of floor plan would make James want to live here? I begin to stack a bunch of boxes to make a wall on the far side of the attic to block out the bags and other assorted items that live over there, out of sight. *There, a nice open space free of clutter.*

Not that James would really care, but this space could use a good cleaning. More to the point, a clean space will minimize the many objections my parents will most likely raise to upend my plan. I need to sell them on this, too, so I head down the stairs, purposely making a lot of noise so the family will know I'm up here. I'm going to make sure the attic isn't an attic anymore. It's a destination.

"Hi, Mom," I say brightly as I stroll through the kitchen and into the mudroom.

"Hi. Um, what are you up to?" she asks while putting away dinner plates.

"Nothing. I just need some cleaning supplies. Where are James and Dad?"

"They're in the family room, watching a game... wait. Cleaning supplies?"

Having found the spray cleaner and a handful of rags, I walk across the kitchen and poke my head into the family room for a little check-in. "Hi, Dad. What're you guys doing?"

"Sox are on," James mumbles, visibly annoyed. "We finally found the remote that you buried in your stupid fort."

"James…" Dad says in a warning voice but then picks up where James left off. "Vivian, can you please clean up some of this stuff sometime? It's impossible to move around in here. Half the couch is covered in blankets."

"I would, Dad, but it's the only place where I can have some quiet time, since James and I share a room," I say, adding the extra flair of dismay.

"Okay, I get that, but can you maybe… downsize a little bit?"

"Maybe." I turn around and skip extra happily up the stairs with rags and spray cleaner.

I can't help but smile as I climb back into the attic. Now that my plan is taking shape, I want James to notice I'm up here so as to pique his curiosity. So I leave the door open just a bit, kind of like leaving a trail of crumbs for a pigeon.

I notice an old desk lamp sticking out of one of the boxes in the far corner and plug it in. It adds a nice glow to the space by the window. The whole room feels better after the window has been open and I've given the place a once-over with the cleaner. I look around, impressed with myself. In less than an hour, I've transformed this forgotten space into a nice little bunk room—like sleepover camp.

Time to set the trap.

I hustle back to my bedroom to grab a bedside table and my iPad. My next move is kind of a risk because once I make it, there may be no going back. I'm not strong enough to move a bed up here alone, but I can manage the beanbag. James loves the beanbag. It's big, puffy, and oh so comfortable, so much so that he can sleep on it. And that lived-in look is precisely what I'm going for. I shove it up the stairs with some effort and stick it over by the window, next to the bedside table and lamp, giving that corner a cozy feel. My lovely little nook even leaves an open space on the other side of the wall that just screams for a mattress to live there, if we get that far.

Okay, it's go time. I practically gallop down the stairs, sounding very excited, like something amazing is going on. I walk into the cramped family room with a big grin on my face like I have a guilty secret and dive into my fort to grab my starry-night mini projector. I pull the plug from the wall and pause to flash my little grin at James.

"What are you doing?" James asks, eyeing the projector and the spring in my step.

"Why don't you come up and see?" I run up the stairs. I need to get up there with enough time to plug in the projector and make a few last-minute adjustments.

I can hear James coming up the stairs, so I plop myself down on the beanbag, looking all chill. He rounds the corner at the top step and stops in his tracks.

"Whoa… What are you doing up here?" James scans the attic, and his gaze eventually settles on me relaxing on the cozy bean bag. I put some books nearby for effect and, even better, have stretched out with my iPad just to show that someone could play a lot of video games up here, uninterrupted.

"I'm making it my new bedroom," I say casually. "Yup. All mine."

"Mom and Dad said it was okay?" he asks, a little puzzled but obviously very curious.

"I didn't ask. I just did it. They're the ones always complaining about my big fort taking up all that space in the family room, so now I'm here. Problem solved. My own little space just for me. I'm happy. They're happy."

It's almost not fair. I can see the wheels turning in James's head.

"But you can still have my room," I say, layering on the sincerity. "I mean, the pink paint color doesn't really look very boyish, but I'm sure you'll get used to it."

James is still looking around the attic, his hand resting on the back of his neck. He looks like his brain hurts.

I pull a warm fleece blanket up over myself and rest my iPad on top of it. *Good time to make an announcement.* "I'm going to play Minecraft all night."

And that does it.

The perplexed expression on James's face gives way to realization, as if he just discovered a baby dinosaur under the floorboards. He's visualizing himself in the privacy of the attic, like he must have it. He asks, "Don't you want to have your own room back? All to yourself?"

Got him!

"Well, I don't know," I say, stretching out on the beanbag, forcing a yawn. "I like it up here. It's private and cozy, and I can do anything I want without anyone coming up to bug me."

At that, I hear footsteps coming up the stairs. It's Mom, with Dad right behind her.

"What are you guys doing up here?" Mom looks around my new bedroom addition. "Well, well, someone's been busy. Is this why you wanted the spray cleaner?"

"Yup," I reply.

"Mm-hmm. Nice job." Mom's eyes rest on me, and with a little bit of suspicion in her voice, she asks, "Now, what is your plan exactly?"

Dad is looking at me expectantly but with a little smile on his face.

"James and I are tired of sharing a room, and you guys are tired of all my stuff living in the family room, so I thought I would create my own space. This is my reading corner. My bed is going over there. I might hang some pictures above it. Oh, and look!"

And that's when I turn out the light and hit them with the projector. The entire attic, in an instant, is transformed into the Milky Way. James's mouth hangs open for a second.

Dad whistles under his breath. "This is pretty awesome, V."

"You're going to let her sleep up here?" James asks, incredulous.

"Wait, I think we need to talk about this first," Mom says, exasperated. She looks over at Dad and says, "I'm not sure about her sleeping up here."

Mom turns to me with her arms crossed. "What if you need to get up in the middle of the night? I wish you had at least asked us about this."

I begin to protest, "But, Mom…"

"It's no big deal, Grace," Dad says, his hands on his hips as he turns to face her. "Let her and James have some privacy. I think it's a great idea."

There is a pause, and for an instant, the room goes quiet as Mom and Dad stare at each other.

Mom is the one to break the silence first. "Yeah, of course you do." She has this weird look on her face—a sort of half smile but mixed with that glare we all try to avoid. She holds her stare at Dad for an extra-long moment and then sort of shrugs while shaking her head, a non-verbal "Whatever."

Dad nods in Mom's direction and turns to me. "We can help you with moving your bed tomorrow, Vivian. But tonight, everyone sleeps in their bedrooms, okay? In fact, it's bedtime right now for both of you."

James and I take turns getting changed in our bedroom, perhaps for the last time. I turn out the light, say, "Good night," and wait.

"Vivian?"

"Yes, brother?"

"That attic room is pretty awesome."

"Yes. Yes, it is."

"Are you sure you don't want to stay here in your room? I mean, you can be right across from the bathroom that way."

I roll my eyes. *The bathroom? Seriously?*

But he just gave me an easy opening, so I turn over and prop myself up on one arm to face him. "Why? Do you want the attic?"

"I do. I mean, it's pretty awesome up there. And then we don't have to worry about always being in each other's way."

This is too easy. "Well, I was kind of excited about having my own space way upstairs. And it's a pretty cool room… but you're right about the bathroom thing. Is that what you want to do? You move upstairs, and I stay here?"

"If you want to do that. Yes."

I wait an extra second to build up the tension before saying, "Well… okay. Yes, let's do it that way."

"Awesome." James jumps out of bed and walks into the hallway to Dad's room.

I smile big and wide as I listen to him explain our new deal to Dad. My room. My space. Just like before. I try to suppress my laughter, wildly kicking my legs under the covers.

Awesome.

CHAPTER SEVEN

FALL TO THE UNFAMILIAR

MY EYES OPEN WITH THE sun streaming into my room. I look over to see James still there, sleeping in the bed next to the other wall. *Did that happen last night? Did I just get James out of my room forever? I didn't dream all that, did I?*

Nope. After breakfast, Dad helps James move his stuff into the attic, but not before presenting me with a new wrinkle in the agreement—we are only going to switch rooms if I move my fort out of the family room. I pretend to make a fuss, but really, that was the plan all along. My fort will now live in my bedroom, just like always. *Perfect.* Everyone's going to be happy in their own spaces.

I take the afternoon to reorganize my room back to the way I like it and happily help James move his clothes to the attic. I get right down to cleaning—even vacuuming!—in an attempt to de-boy my room.

Finally, after all the moving, cleaning, and reorganizing, I get to lie down on my bed, back in my own room, and it sparkles. It's been a good day. My only thought as I turn off the light next to my bed is about when I should rebuild my fort. I think I'll wait a week to get used to the delightful openness of my space. I roll onto my side, curl up with my stuffed animals, and happily drift off to sleep.

* * *

Later on, a sudden jolt rips me from my warm, cozy dream state. Seemingly faraway noises make me sit up in my bed and look toward the door. James is standing in the hallway.

"What's going on?" I ask.

"Shush," he says but not in the usual mean way. No, it's more of a warning, protective.

I get out of bed and creep out to the hallway to stand next to James. Barefoot, we pad carefully along the hallway carpet to the top of the stairs. I can hear Mom and Dad more clearly now, arguing in low whispers, and Mom sounds like she's crying. From up here, it's hard to understand what they're saying, but they sound mad and sad at the same time. James and I sit down on the top step, not saying anything. I'm trying to understand what this could possibly be about.

Suddenly, Mom's voice rises, but then Dad's drowns hers out. Shouting replaces low whispers. They never shout, always trying to hide their fights. It's as if Mom and Dad all of a sudden chose to stop being quiet—to stop not talking to each other or around each other. The effect is shocking, like a soccer ball knocking the wind out of me.

I put my hands over my ears. The tears that slip between my fingers mix with my hair. But still, I can hear them. I can't block out the yelling, no matter how hard I try. James's forehead rests on his crossed arms over his knees. He's crying too. Sure, it has been uncomfortable in the house for a long time, but we've never heard them fight like this before.

Something falls to the floor and shatters loudly, making me sit upright out of my little protective ball.

Out of nowhere, James lifts his head and screams, "Stop it! Stop it!"

The house is suddenly quiet. A cold, frozen kind of quiet. I sit there, holding my breath, afraid to move.

Footsteps pass the landing below us, and I hear keys being picked up from the front table in the hallway. The door opens, and the footsteps move to the front porch. Someone just left and closed the front door behind them.

Wait… Someone just left.

"James?" I whisper, gulping back tears.

He looks at me but doesn't say anything. We stay at the top of the steps, not knowing what to do or say.

Mom appears at the bottom step and puts her hand to her mouth. She climbs the stairs to sit with us on the floor and hugs us for what feels like a very long time. The shoulder of my pajama top slowly gets wet with Mom's tears as she holds me quietly. I want all of this to stop. I want to get away, but I need my mom too. So I just sit here, feeling so uncertain.

Mom takes a deep breath. "I'm so sorry you had to hear that, James, Vivian. Dad and I love you both very much, but we just aren't… We aren't happy with each other right now."

"Where is Daddy? Where did he go?" I ask.

"I don't know, honey." This makes Mom cry more. She says through tears, "I think to your grandparents' house."

"I want to see him," James says. "I want to call him."

"You will, honey. You will, but not tonight. I'm so sorry."

James stands up, breaking away from Mom, and goes upstairs to his room in the attic, leaving the two of us alone. This is all too much for me. My stomach hurts like I'm going to be sick. I have to get to the bathroom, so I pull away. I barely make it in time, with Mom coming in right behind me as I throw up my dinner. She sits next to me, the two of us crying together, until my tummy is empty.

Mom helps me back into bed and tucks me in. She sits with me for a while, rubbing my back, trying to settle me down. I lie in my bed, feeling nothing anymore except the tears still falling down my face, before I eventually fall asleep.

The next day, Mom is on the phone with Dad a few times, talking about whatever happened last night. James and I are in a strange suspended state of not understanding any of it. The best place for me is either outside or in my room, away from everyone. But as Dad's car pulls into the driveway, I realize that I can't hide from this. He and Mom want to talk to me and James.

The four of us sit together in the family room, and I just know this isn't good. Dad is looking at me, almost like it's all he can do. His eyes are so sad.

"Kids, your dad and I are really sorry about what happened last night," Mom says. Her eyes are puffy and glazed, and her cheeks are red. Her hands are clasped together, clutching a wet ball of tissue.

Dad looks at us. "Sometimes your mom and I don't get along, and we'll argue about things... but we're really sorry that you heard all of that. Um..." He puts his hand to his mouth, swallows hard, and looks at Mom.

My tummy starts to hurt again, but I fight through the wave of nausea. I haven't eaten anything all day anyway. The horrible part of this whole thing is that Mom and Dad obviously have something to tell us, but it's like they don't even know who should speak when. The tension between them is brutal.

And just out of the blue, James, who has been sitting quietly next to me, asks the question that has haunted us all day—longer actually. "Are you getting a divorce?"

That word hangs there over us like a weight in the air. The room feels small and tight. I look down and notice that my hands are trembling and tears have been falling down my face onto my lap. I'm not even sure when I started to cry. I just keep looking at my hands, hoping they'll stop shaking. *Why are they shaking? How is this happening?*

Mom reaches over to hold my hands in hers. Dad does the same to James, sliding over on the couch to be closer to him.

Then Mom says what I desperately hoped not to hear. "Yes."

That single, simple word unleashes so much sadness in me. My tears fall in a wave now as I begin to cry uncontrollably. A year's worth of worry bursting out of me. Neither James nor I say anything. What can I say at a moment like this? It's all too much to process.

But there isn't time for that because Mom says a little too quickly, "Dad and I want you to know this is not your fault. We love you both very much."

Dad is nodding.

Why would they even say that to us? We aren't the ones fighting. But actually, I don't know what to think, and I start to wonder if they really mean it. A sudden thought occurs to me. *Is it possible that we have a part in all this?*

I look over at James. He looks so sad, and a single tear rolls down his face.

"You guys have to know this," Dad says. "Just because Mommy and I don't want to… I mean, we can't be together… right now. That doesn't mean that we don't love you very much."

They do love us, he goes on to say, and then he explains some plan about how they're going to live close to each other so that James and I can see both of them every week.

Wait. I have friends whose parents are divorced, so I know a little bit about how some of these things work. But honestly, Mom and Dad really suck at explaining this. I can feel my face getting red as I try, quite unsuccessfully, to get my head around this.

"You mean, you're going to live somewhere else, Dad?" I ask.

He looks at Mom, who says, "No, honey. I am."

"What?"

What?

The words just hang there. *Mom's leaving. She is going to live somewhere else. Without us.*

Dad breaks into my thoughts, saying, "You kids and I are going to stay here in our house as I continue to work from home, at least for this school year. You'll get to see Mom every week for dinners some nights after school and on a bunch of weekends too. I mean, when her work allows for that."

Mom flinches at that comment and looks down at her feet.

Dad goes on. "I know… I mean, your mom and I know this is a lot to take in right now, but we want to make it work for you. Find a way to make this new normal, um… better."

Mom is still looking at her feet, not blinking, and she nods as Dad says that last part. I don't know what she thinks he means by all that. I certainly can't figure it out.

The rest of the conversation is a blur because I'm too overwhelmed to hear anything else. Both Mom and Dad hold on to me, saying they love me and always will. But is that really the point right now? They might think so, but I don't. My family as I know it just got obliterated with an answer to a question in one simple word—*yes*. I can't understand it all. Not at this moment anyway.

And even the whole arrangement of it all is so weird. Mom is moving out. She is leaving *us*. That's totally backward compared to most kids I know with divorced parents. Normally, they live with their moms, go to school, and visit their dads on nights and weekends. But with us, it's flipped. It's the opposite. Just another totally not-normal twist in my family during a year with no normal anywhere.

A little later, James and I sit together in my room with the door closed, not saying much. Mom and Dad are still in the kitchen, talking. God knows about what. Maybe something like, *Gee, I think that went really well, Grace. Me, too, Jim.*

Well, it didn't. Of course, it didn't. Does it ever?

I find myself staring at James because I don't know what else to do. He's just looking out the window, lost in thought.

CHAPTER EIGHT

GIRL PARTY

MY iPAD DINGS JUST AS I'm getting ready for bed. A month has passed since that terrible night with my parents, but I'm still not used to going to sleep without saying good night to Mom. Sometimes Katie will secretly FaceTime me right before we go to sleep to cheer me up. Usually, we speak in whispers, but this evening, Katie is sitting up in her bed, lights on all around her and a huge grin on her face.

"You'll never guess what we're doing tomorrow!" she says.

I turn the volume down on my iPad, so her voice doesn't carry down the stairs to where James and Dad are sitting. I know that big toothy smile and those water-blue eyes mean something fun is just around the corner. I sit up straight. "Well? Tell me!"

Katie giggles. "I am so psyched. Lucy's mom said we could all go to their house tomorrow night for an outdoor distance party! Just us GirlZ and the moms!"

"Really?" I say too loudly.

Dad yells up at me to shut it down and go to sleep.

"Sorry, Dad. Okay."

I bury myself and my iPad under the heavy comforter so no one can hear me then lower my voice to a whisper. "I'm supposed to see Mom tomorrow night. It's her night for us."

Katie is nodding. "Uh-huh. I know. But my mom called your mom to make sure you could both come. It's all set! Girl party!"

Girl party. The first in what feels like forever. I'm so excited, I can hardly fall asleep.

Dad confirms the plan the next day. "I'm going to watch James's baseball game tonight, so you and Mom get to hang out with all of your friends. How's that sound?"

"Amazing."

"You have to wear masks the entire time, and is it possible for you girls to maintain some distance and not hug each other all night?"

That's a good question because we GirlZ are all big huggers. But I'm so excited about the party that I promise to be good.

Dad and James are tripping over each other, getting ready to leave, as Mom drives in. She parks and waits for me at the end of the driveway. I skip down the front steps and run into a warm Mom hug—one of the many things I miss so much without her here.

"Ready to go?" she asks.

"Totally! I'm glad Dad and James are doing their own thing tonight." I feel a little awkward saying that out loud, but it's the truth. "I'm glad it's just us and just girls at the party."

Mom smiles at me as we start to walk hand in hand. "Me too. All-girl parties are the best." A few seconds pass, then she asks, "How's art going? I haven't seen your work in a while."

"I finally finished that painting I was working on, the one of the girl with the flowers in her hair. I love it. My art teacher said it's amazing."

"I think you're pretty amazing, too, Vivian. I'd like to see that painting sometime, okay?"

"Yes, definitely. Next time I, um, come over to your... What do you call it? Is it a house?"

"More of a condo, I guess." Mom stops walking to turn and look at me. "Listen, Vivian, I want to tell you something." Her eyes are fixed on mine. "I am so proud of you in every way. I mean, in everything you do."

I nod, unsure what to say. I hope Mom doesn't want to talk about feelings right now. I want to go to the party, not think about her and Dad.

She adds, "I know this is a really tough time for you and James."

Here we go.

"It hurts your dad and me to think of how upsetting all of this is—us not being together, the virus, remote school. But I see a lot of strength in you, honey. You just keep doing what you do, and you don't let anything stop you. I wish I had that much strength in me sometimes."

That last part catches me by surprise. "But, Mom, I got all of that strength from you."

Mom raises an eyebrow, which she always does when she's amused at something I said or when she has a question. In this case, it's both. "What do you mean by that?"

"I don't know, but it's just how you are. Don't you have to be strong, and even brave, to be a doctor?"

A bit about Mom: she grew up in a small town in Virginia with two brothers, and she often says that having two brothers was a lot of fun. I don't know how fun it would be to have two brothers—one is plenty on the annoying scale. But Mom says that while the boys always got into trouble, Nana and Pop would think Mom was like an angel.

How do I get that *vibe going in my house?*

Mom always says growing up in a small town was nice in many ways. She always spent summers outdoors, making up her own fun with her friends or brothers in the fields, ponds, and woods near their home. Sometimes, she just liked to go out on hikes by herself along the trails. Pop loves to tell the story about how Mom became a hero when she was fifteen while on one of those hikes.

Mom was out with her dog one afternoon and saw smoke coming from the barn behind the house on her neighbor's property. As she got closer for a look inside, she saw that a fire had broken out by the workbench and was spreading quickly.

Six horses lived in the stable inside the barn, and they were scared, kicking against their stalls and neighing—more like screaming—loudly. Mom called out for help, but nobody answered. The sound the horses made was terrifying, and the fire was spreading toward the stalls. She looked around and realized no one else was coming. So Mom ran into the barn, jumped over the fire that was burning on the floorboards, and started lifting the latches of the stalls to let the horses out.

The fire was moving fast, and the smoke was burning her eyes. The last horse was panicking and wouldn't come out of its stall. It reared back from Mom, its eyes wide with fear. She tried to wave it out, but the horse resisted and thrashed about.

Mom was out of time and also running out of breath because of the smoke. It was getting hard to see. Her eyes were watering, and she was coughing. She had to get out of the barn.

Mom was running toward the door when, all of a sudden, the scared horse crashed out of its stall, ran past her, and knocked her through the air, smashing her against the wall before she fell to the ground.

Mom lay there, not quite able to move. Her forearm was badly broken, and she was dazed from the fall, feeling like she was in a type of strange dream. She knew something was wrong, but she'd taken such a hit from the horse that her body wasn't ready to move yet.

The hay by her feet had caught fire, and that shook her to consciousness. Mom started to half stumble, half crawl. She made it just outside the barn door before she fell to her knees and crawled to a safe spot away from the fire.

Mom says she doesn't remember what happened after that or how long she was lying there. The next thing she knew, she was in Pop's arms while he carried her home. The barn had burned to the ground.

Mom's heroism landed her on the front page of the local paper, with a picture of her standing next to the neighbors and the local fire chief. She had her arm in a sling and a smile on her face. All the horses were okay because Mom had been so brave. Nana and Pop keep that picture in a frame in the kitchen by the phone. Mom doesn't talk about it much, but she really was a hero that day.

Pop says he wasn't ever the least bit surprised that Mom was brave enough to run into that burning barn. "I'm just glad we got her back," he would say, looking at the picture. His words would trail off as he shook his head.

Mom and I walk on as she smiles and says, "Yes, that's true, V. I have to be strong—and, I guess, brave—in my work every day, but sometimes, it still makes me tired."

"You taught me how to chase away bad thoughts. To close my eyes, be still, and breathe. That is what helped me stay calm when I once lost Buster."

"You lost Buster?"

I tell Mom the whole story about Buster taking off on Mia and me in the woods that day.

"That's quite a scare," she says. "I'm not surprised that you were brave enough to stay calm. Um, what did Dad say when you got home?"

"Oh, I never told him—or anyone actually."

Oops.

Mom just smiles at me. "You're something else, Vivian."

Whatever that means.

We're the last mother-daughter pair to arrive at Lucy's house, and the GirlZ are already running around, playing soccer. As we step into the backyard, everyone makes a big fuss with air-kisses and sing-song greetings from the moms. We GirlZ haven't seen each other as a group since that warm spring day when we went for ice cream. Having all of us together again feels like a homecoming of lost friends. A big cleansing exhalation of loneliness leaves my body. I notice that all the moms are hugging each other.

"Distance, pleeease!" we GirlZ shout in mock scolding at this flagrant violation of distance rules.

They respond with happy laughter mixed with apologies, hands in the air. Mom's smiling, but her eyes are moist with tears. Grown-ups are weird.

"Girls, head on over to the little corner we set up for y'all over there." Lucy's mom points with her chin toward the far corner across the yard. "Lucy, you bring the snacks, and, Miss Vivian, will you please carry the tray of lemonade and cups, honey?"

Dr. G is so nice. She always calls me Miss Vivian. Lucy says it's a Southern thing. I like it.

Four colorful beach chairs are set up in Lucy's big sandbox next to her playset. Her backyard is huge, with a zipline and climbing pegs set up on trees. The snacks take priority over climbing every time, of course, so we sit down in our backyard beach paradise and dive in.

The moms on the deck have already helped themselves to the wine, like always, and are chit-chatting in Mom's direction. Their laughter and happy talk have been replaced by looks of concern mixed with encouraging smiles. I bet they're talking about Mom and Dad. They always do that. Just when everyone gets together to have some fun, grown-ups find reasons to get all serious. It's annoying, and it makes me feel kind of quiet.

I think Lucy notices my change in mood, because she throws a Starburst pack at me, which bounces off my head.

"Where's Lexi?" Mia asks.

"She went for a bike ride with her friend Hannah," Lucy says with hands in the air, blocking my return volley of popcorn. "That was a little while ago, so she may be back in a bit."

I'm glad to hear that. I like Lexi. She is really cool for an eighth grader. Some older brothers and sisters—like mine and Mia's—are not very nice to their younger siblings, but not Lexi. She's always nice to us GirlZ when we're over, and she's been especially nice to me lately. I'm secretly a little jealous of how close she and Lucy are—very different from my annoying, gross sibling.

Apparently, Mia is thinking the same thing. She blurts, "Can we trade sisters please, Lucy?"

"Oh, and *any* of you can have James!" I look around. "Anyone?"

No takers. Dang it.

Mia's sister-swap request reminds me of something else. "It was so funny watching you two fight on FaceTime the other day."

Mia pauses in the middle of whatever story she's telling and gives me the sideways evil eye. "Vivian…"

"No, seriously, this was you: 'Blah, blah, boy thing. Blah, blah, school thing. Blah, blah, clothes thing.' And then Emma noisily barged into the kitchen where you were sitting, and you got all huffy…"

"*First* of all, know *this*," Mia announces. "I do *not* 'blah, blah, blah…'"

"Oh yes, you do!" Katie chimes in with a mouthful of Skittles. "Blah, blah, *drama,* blah!"

Mia throws a handful of popcorn at her, pretending to be mad even though she's laughing.

I laugh even harder then say, "And then Mia puts our FaceTime on mute, and she starts yelling at Emma and wildly gesturing at her, which is super hilarious in silent-movie mode!"

I, of course, imitate them, waving my arms at my pretend iPad with dramatic, silent expressions. Everyone jumps in, doing their own version of silent sister fighting at Mia, who throws more popcorn, this time in my direction.

Time flies by as it always does in carefree mode. We GirlZ transition from snack wars and giggle fits to barefoot soccer and, eventually, dinner. Dr. G puts out burgers, dogs, and delicious BBQ chicken for us to help ourselves to. I notice that the moms are all finally having fun, lightened up by time spent together and freely flowing, easy laughter. The firepit illuminates us all as we balance watermelon slices on paper plates and hold cups of lemonade. Girl party. Friends being together. It's a special moment for sure.

And then, as moments tend to do, things change quickly when Lexi barges in through the gate to the backyard, sees me sitting there, and yells, "Vivian, my little soccer sisterrr! Is that you, girl?"

She lifts me out of my chair with a big hug and spins me around, causing watermelon rinds to fly through the air like one-way boomerangs. All the GirlZ shriek and laugh while ducking flying fruit.

Lucy's mom, with a mixture of annoyance and amusement, yells, "Girls! Distance, please! Come on, Lexi, you nutcake! Y'all just crazy these days!"

This makes us all laugh harder. We're literally falling out of our chairs as Lexi yells back, "Mom! 'Nutcake'? Who even says that?"

And the moms crack up too.

Eventually, it's time to head home. As Mom and I begin to say our goodbyes, the other GirlZ disappear into the house for a quick moment and return with a present for me—a beautiful painting by Lucy. It's a wild mixture of orange, white, pink, and red in the shape of a heart that seems to float above the canvas. It has four rings around it—one for each of the GirlZ. At the bottom of the painting, it reads, "We love you forever," and it's signed by Lucy, Katie, and Mia.

Lucy gives me a big hug, and so does Dr. G, who smiles at me and says, "I know it's a tough time right now for you, Miss Vivian, but you stay strong. You'll get through this. I just know you will, honey. Strong is what you are."

Mom and I walk home in the dark. The path is lit by the occasional streetlamp and the moon above us. It's so quiet even though it's not that late. I turn Lucy's painting over to look at it under the lamp's glow. It's beautiful.

Mom asks, "Did you have fun tonight, V?"

Why do parents ask questions about things they already know the answer to? "Yes, Mom. It was amazing. What about you?"

"Oh… It was really great to see everyone again. We always laugh when we moms get together, and I enjoy seeing you play with Mia, Lucy, and Katie."

"And drinking wine."

"Oh, stop."

"What? It's true! Every time you *moms* get together on the deck, you drink wine. I mean, like every. Single. Time."

Mom's laughing now. "All right, fine. Yes, we like wine… but not *all* the time."

"You drink coffee too."

"Well, of course. Coffee is what makes the day actually happen."

"And apparently, so does wine."

Mom laughs in mock exasperation. "You're too young to know these things!"

We walk on in silence, holding hands. My mind returns to seeing the moms on the deck, having their group-therapy session.

"What do all of you talk about?" I ask.

"What do you talk about?" she asks.

"I asked you first."

Mom looks at me, and before she can say anything, I say quietly, "You talk about Dad, don't you?"

"Yes. Yes, we do, honey."

"What do you say?"

"Well… I told the moms about what Dad and I are going through now and where the future may take us.

I talk about being sad too. Things are just kind of, um, uncertain right now."

"If you're sad, then why are you doing this?"

"It's not *me* doing this, Vivian." Mom stops walking and turns to face me, hands on hips.

"It's *us*. Dad *and* me!"

I don't want a fight, and I look down at my feet. "I didn't mean it that way. I just wish you and Dad could be happy again. Go back to how things used to be."

Mom goes quiet, as if she's gathering herself. She takes a deep breath and puts her arm around me. "I'm sorry, V. I didn't mean to say that… like that. Your dad and I wish that we could have stayed together. But we have tried many times to… well, fix us, and I guess we just ran out of ideas about what to try next. Talking to my friends helps me organize it all in my head because there is a lot to think about, and sometimes saying it out loud helps things become clearer and easier to understand. Does that make sense to you?"

"Yes, I think so." My mind wanders back to what we GirlZ talked about tonight. It wasn't about my mom and dad at all. We mostly just talked about silly school things, soccer, and just stuff—most of it hilarious.

But at one point, Lucy told us a little bit about her life in Florida for the first time, saying that she lost her dad when she was six. He went for a run one day, like every other day, and got hit by a car. He died at the hospital before anyone could even see him. It's been Lucy, Lexi, and their mom ever since. I didn't really know what to say, so I reached for her hand and squeezed it. Lucy turned and gave me a little smile. Sometimes you don't even need to say anything to be a friend. You just have to be there at the right moment. Kind of like what Mom just said.

CHAPTER NINE

WHEN I GROW UP

L AST FALL, THE SCHOOL YEAR started out with a weird hybrid schedule where I was Zooming for class one week and sitting in a classroom the next. But at least I was able to see the GirlZ while at school because we are all in the same cohort. This is an in-school week, and my classroom is buzzing with the higher-than-usual energy kids get when we're together in person.

Ms. Doodle stands at the front of the class to settle everyone down. "All right, my loves! Time to get started."

Conversations mixed with the sound of shuffling chairs and desk drawers opening and closing begin to fade as Ms. Doodle nods her approval. "Okay, who can tell me how many days until opening day?"

Everyone's hands shoot into the air. Ms. Doodle likes to start class with some kind of trivia question. She's a huge Red Sox fan and counting down to opening day at Fenway Park is one of her favorites, so we always know to be ready for it.

Mia almost knocks her notepad and pens off her desk with excitement. Ms. Doodle smiles and says, "Let's have it, Miss Mia."

"Eleven days!"

"Well done!" Ms. Doodle hands Mia a Red Sox sticker. "Bonus question." Ms. Doodle holds up a Red Sox foam finger, a highly coveted prize. "Against who?"

Hands shoot up again, but then a few drop back down hesitantly. Ms. Doodle surveys the class, building the tension.

"Sir Tyler, what'cha got?"

From the back of the room, Tyler shouts out, "Baltimore!"

"Nope! Wrong answer!"

This sends the classroom into a buzz.

"No looking at your phones over there!" Ms. Doodle shouts at a group of other boys. "Anyone? This is a foam-finger-worthy bonus prize. I'll give you a hint—rhymes with 'plays.'"

After a second's pause, hands shoot back up with a burst of chatter.

"Go ahead, Alice," Ms. Doodle says as she waves the foam finger in the air.

"The Rays?" Alice says.

"Whoo-hoo!" Ms. Doodle shouts. "Foam finger for you, my love!"

Ms. Doodle is the best. Her sense of humor is a little crazy, and I think that's the glue that holds learning and fun together. We all need healthy doses of crazy and fun with the strangeness of distance rules, mask wearing, and only half of us being in school at one time.

This week's assignment is to think about what we want to be when we grow up and be ready to speak about it in front of the class. I ask Ms. Doodle if I can go to the library to do a little research. "Of course, Vivian. That's a great idea. But be back in twenty minutes, okay?"

I grab my backpack and walk down the hallway, thinking about future me, until I'm rudely interrupted by two boys running by me at full speed, making all kinds of noise and acting like, well, typical boys.

"Ouch! Watch it!" I say.

"*You* watch it, Viviaaan," Jonathan chirps in his obnoxious, mocking voice as he barges into me.

Argh, I can't stand him! He's in the other fifth-grade class and is super annoying.

As I turn the corner at the entrance to the library, two other boys come running down the hall at top speed. All four of them crash into each other, playing some kind of tag, screeching, and wrestling—or more like clumsy air-boxing.

Apparently, the librarian, Ms. Huffle, thinks the boys are pretty annoying too. I would bet people can hear her a mile away as she rounds on them and yells, "You boys *stop* what you are doing right *now*! Jonathan, you get over here!"

All four boys freeze. *Busted.*

I never knew Ms. Huffle had such a loud voice. She *is* a librarian after all, but she quickly lowers the volume to something more like whisper-screaming at the boys about making such a racket during school. I make a snarky face at Jonathan as I pass by. *So satisfying.*

For my assignment, I'm kind of stuck between wanting to be an actor and a lawyer. I know they're two totally different things. I was talking it over with Dad last night at dinner, and he laughed a little bit when I told him. That made me mad, so I threw a green bean at him.

After ducking my green bean, Dad said, "I'm not laughing at your choices because they are bad or even silly, V. I am laughing because I think they're perfect!"

I just looked at him with my snarl face.

"Did you know that some really great lawyers have to be good at acting?"

That got my attention. "What do you mean?"

"Well, let's say that you're a public defender—someone who helps a person who has been accused of a crime—present their side of the story in court. You have to build a case, highlight the important points, and present it to a judge or jury. Like memorizing your lines. I think you would be a great lawyer because you're really good at, um, arguing. Believe me, I know. I mean, I'm glad that you speak up when you feel strongly about something. That's a good thing."

"Then why do you always tell me to stop arguing and just do what you say?"

"That's called parenting, honey. It's different."

Whatever.

Having wandered into the library all alone while Ms. Huffle deals with Jonathan and his gang of misfits, I'm not totally sure where to begin. So I poke around the book stacks, looking at the titles and wondering where the law section is. *Is there a law section? There has to be, right?*

Out of the corner of my eye, I see Ms. Huffle return to her desk. As she sits down, she takes a deep breath. I bet she gave those boys a shellacking.

From behind one of the book stacks, I offer a cheery, "Hi, Ms. Huffle."

"Oh, my goodness!" She practically jumps out of her seat. "You scared me! Don't you know not to sneak up on people?"

She was smoothing her dress as I said hello, but now her hands are pressed on her thighs, almost clutching. Her face is kind of red too.

"I'm sorry… um, I came in to find a book, and I was looking at all of these stacks."

Obviously, this is not a good time for Ms. Huffle. It's probably not going to be a good time for me either.

Ms. Huffle pulls herself together. "Okay. Yes. What book are you looking for?" She stands up and starts to walk toward the stacks with me.

"I was looking for something about being a public defender. Can you tell me where the law section is?"

Ms. Huffle turns to look at me, peering down her nose at the top of my head. She flattens her wiry hair with both hands. "Public defender? Where did you ever learn that word?"

It occurs to me that I don't know Ms. Huffle very well. This is totally awkward.

"What grade are you in?" she asks.

My face is getting hot, and I start to feel silly for even being here. "I'm in fifth grade. In Ms. Doodle's class, and I'm hoping to learn about being a lawyer someday."

Ms. Huffle looks like she's sizing me up—for what, I don't know. But she abruptly turns me around and walks me to the other side of the library near the study corner. "I don't know about books on being a lawyer, but here is one that might help you think about what you want to be when you grow up."

I look at the cover of the book that Ms. Huffle just handed me. It's so lame, like a picture book for younger kids. I'm not getting anywhere, and apparently, Ms. Huffle isn't in the mood to help. So I quietly sign out the book, turn and walk out the way I came in. Not a very happy library experience.

I return to the sanctuary of my homeroom with Ms. Doodle and sit down at my desk in time for the next lesson. I feel stupid about walking away basically empty-handed with nothing but a little kids' book to look at. But I'm madder that I didn't stick up for myself—that I just got embarrassed and left. That bothers me the most. I sit through the next lesson, fuming, not really hearing Ms. Doodle.

As we're getting ready to leave for the day, Ms. Doodle stops by my desk. "Hi, Vivian. What's up for the afternoon?"

"I don't know. I think I have soccer."

Ms. Doodle can always tell when something is bothering me. She stands there, eyes smiling at me above her mask, as she waits for me to say something else. I'm not sure if I'll be able to do this assignment, and I don't want to fail. So I tell her the entire story, layering on the details about Ms. Huffle's grumpiness. Ms. Doodle doesn't really comment on that, which is kind of disappointing.

I was hoping she would come to my defense against Ms. Huffle and call the principal to get the evil librarian fired or something.

Instead, Ms. Doodle asks, "So, what are you going to do now?"

This is a question Ms. Doodle often asks when we talk about something that's bothering me. When my parents started not getting along, she would walk with me at recess and ask about things at home. I don't normally like to talk to grown-ups about my feelings, but Ms. Doodle always makes it easy for me. And this time, I already have an answer for her.

"Well, I want to go back and try to get a real book that might actually help me."

Ms. Doodle smiles. "That's a good answer, Vivian. Maybe there's another way to learn about being a lawyer. Perhaps you should get a book about the Constitution. That's where all the laws in our country started. Let's go back to the library and try again. I'll come with you."

So I grab my backpack, and we walk down the hall together without talking. I keep my eyes on the ground in front of me as my inner reel replays the episode with Ms. Huffle. My arms are crossed tightly around my chest as I imagine what I'm going to tell her she can do with this stupid book. *Why don't you take this little kids' book and—*

"Did you just say something, Vivian?" Ms. Doodle asks, snapping me back to reality.

"Huh? No, I don't think so."

"Oh. You were just mumbling something."

I really need to learn to keep my fume-thinking on mute.

Ms. Huffle is sitting at her desk, looking like she finally got her wiry hair under control. Actually, her whole face looks more under control. She even smiles as she looks up and says to Ms. Doodle, "Hi, Michelle. Oh, I see you have your student here with you. We met earlier today when she wanted to figure out what she wants to be when she grows up."

Huh?

She's smiling at me. It's a warm, encouraging smile.

Okay. On the one hand, maybe she's trying to be nice, but on the other hand, I think maybe she changed her tune just because my teacher is with me. I'm not going to be fooled by that old trick.

"I already know what I want to be—a lawyer. The book you gave me isn't very helpful, and I want another one," I say in my best serious, grown-up voice.

"Um, Vivian, why don't you tell us what it is you want to learn about?" Ms. Doodle says. I think she might be trying to help me not get mad or into trouble.

"I want to learn about the Constitution," I say a bit more politely. "Do you have any books on that?"

Oddly, Ms. Huffle's smile gets even bigger. "Well, certainly. That's a subject we have plenty of books about. Good for you for wanting to understand something as important as that." She stands up and leads me to a shelf where there are all kinds of books about social science and government for different ages.

"This is one of the more advanced books we have." She looks at Ms. Doodle then back at me. "I think it's just right for you. Why don't you take it out and let me know what you think?"

Huh. This is unexpected. She's pretty nice. I don't get it...

Ms. Huffle goes on. "That was you who walked into the library while I had to quiet those boys down. I'm sorry that I didn't hear what you were asking for. I was still so startled from all the noise they were making."

Wait. That was the problem earlier. Of course... the running around. The roughhousing. The boys... so annoying.

I sign the book out and say a more sincere thank-you to the new Ms. Huffle. Ms. Doodle walks with me to the front door of the school.

"Thanks for your help, Ms. Doodle."

"Oh, I didn't do anything, Vivian. I think it's great that you want to learn about the law. Sometimes, you have to think about asking for something you want but perhaps in a different way. In fact, that might be a good thing for a lawyer to remember." She's smiling at me, and I know she's right.

I lean into the double doors, and sunlight fills the school hallway. Ms. Doodle looks outside where the GirlZ are all waiting for me at the bottom of the steps, backpacks on, ready for the walk home.

"Looks like you have a bit of an entourage," she says with a smile. "Have fun at soccer today, and let me know what you think about the book."

I start down the steps and smile over my shoulder. "Thank you. I will."

Mia is staring intently at something on her phone. She taps off a text and looks up to greet me. "Hi, V! What was that all about?"

As we start to walk home, I tell the GirlZ about my library ordeal.

"Ms. Huffle is usually pretty nice to me when I need a book," Katie says. "I'm sure it was the boys who stressed her out." Katie and Jonathan are in the same class, so she knows all about his antics. She takes a sip from her water bottle. "Jonathan never came back to class today. I heard that Ms. Huffle sent him to the principal's office, and they called his mom to come get him."

"Hmpf," Mia says. "I'll bet his parents have a reserved parking space next to the principal's office because they have to come and get him so often."

Lucy looks at me with a curious expression on her face. "I didn't know you wanted to be a lawyer."

"Well, I think so." I explain the acting connection on the walk home.

Lucy nods along with a little grin, but she doesn't say anything.

Katie blurts, "I wrote that I want to be a professional soccer player."

"Shocker!" we say at the same time, all dramatic.

"You guys want to meet up for ice cream this afternoon?" Mia asks, of course, setting up some fun time on our social calendars.

"Katie and I have soccer practice today, but maybe after?" I say.

Everyone agrees to ask the moms—or in my case, Dad—and set up a meeting place. Ice cream with the GirlZ after soccer practice is something to look forward to.

CHAPTER TEN

LUCY'S SECRET

D AD'S FINE WITH THE IDEA of ice-cream after soccer. He and Katie's mom say we can ride our bikes to practice then meet Lucy and Mia at the ice-cream shop afterward.

"And please don't get a massive milkshake or something like that, Vivian. I would like you to leave some room in your tummy for dinner this evening."

"Okay, Dad."

We'll see about that. I love chocolate milkshakes. They make me happy.

Practice goes along like it always does—shooting drills, passing drills, my dad being too loud, and finally, a scrimmage. It's hot out too. All the better for a huge chocolate milkshake with extra chocolate syrup and whipped cream—oh, and sprinkles. That's what I'm dreaming about as Katie and I pedal our bikes out of the parking lot after practice. But Dad calls us back, further delaying my eighteen-ounce chocolate satisfaction.

"Girls, I just got back-to-back texts from Mia's and Lucy's moms," he says, frowning at his phone. "I guess neither one of them can meet you for ice cream."

That's weird. "Did they say why?"

"Nope. Nothing. Just two different texts, both saying the girls can't make it. If you two want to go ahead, that's fine with me. Just come on home after, okay?"

Katie and I look at each other, shrug, and start to pedal into town.

"Maybe their parents had plans for them that they didn't know about," Katie says.

"Both of them?" I ask. "I guess, maybe, but that's kind of random."

"Yeah. It's not like Mia to miss an opportunity to get out of the house," she says as we ride side by side.

It's probably not a big deal. Besides, as Katie devours ice cream and I dig into, yes, a massive tricked-out chocolate milkshake, the curious little voices in my head begin to fade away, replaced by a delicious-food coma. Ice cream always makes everything better.

When I get home, I kick off my soccer cleats and leave my sweaty socks and shin guards on the floor of the mudroom for someone else to deal with.

"Seriously, Vivian?" Dad says. "Come on." He's not happy with my sloppiness lately, and he reminds me he isn't the housemaid—one of his standard lines.

I say, "Sorry," and throw the rest of my gear into the hamper, which is overflowing again.

After being away from my iPad all afternoon, I'm certain there will be a bunch of messages from Lucy and Mia, complaining about their parents messing up today's plans or something like that. So before getting into the shower, I sit on my bed and open up my iPad to find… nothing. Not a single text. Okay, now that is weird.

So I text Katie: *Hear anything from L&M???*

Katie: *Nope. Shrug emoji.*

I send a group GirlZ text just to see what's going on.

Me: *Hi GirlZ! L&M, you missed an amazing ice cream run today!! Ice cream emoji, milkshake emoji. Hungry smiley emoji. Where were you guys??*

I hit Send and hop into the shower, a little distracted but certain I'll get word back any second—especially from Mia, who is always attached to her phone. I towel off, put on my clean clothes, and check my iPad again.

No new messages.

"Vivian, can you please come down here and set the table?" Dad calls from the bottom of the stairs.

I need to build up a little goodwill after the sweaty-soccer-equipment-left-on-the-floor incident, so I head downstairs to the kitchen to help Dad. I eat my dinner quickly, thinking about the GirlZ the whole time and wondering what the heck is going on. Right after I finish putting away the dishes, my tablet dings with a FaceTime request.

It's Lucy. Finally. She's calling from her room, sitting on her bed. Her freckles are more red than usual, which is saying something, and her eyes look tired or sad or both.

What the…?

"Hi!" I say more cheerfully than I'm feeling—somewhat annoyed at not hearing from her all day after she ghosted us for ice cream. "What happened today? Why didn't you come for ice cream?"

Lucy offers a weak smile. "Yeah. I'm sorry. I, um… Well, have you talked to Mia at all?"

Interesting question. "No, I haven't heard from either of you until now. Are you guys okay? What's the matter?"

"I don't know if I can talk about it, Vivian… I don't want things to get worse, but… well, it's about Mia. We had kind of a fight today."

That catches me by surprise. Lucy doesn't fight, or at least, I've never seen her get angry at anyone ever.

"About what?"

"Mia said something really mean at school, and I don't know if I can forgive her." Lucy pauses. "She shared something that I told her once in secret, and it's really personal." Lucy looks away from the screen, biting her lip. It's quivering just a little as she takes a deep breath.

"Lucy, do you want to tell me about it?"

She looks at me, uncertain.

I add, "You can if you want to."

Lucy places her hands under her chin, and tears begin to roll slowly down her face, making streaks over her freckles as she stares off at something. I wait.

Fortunately, quiet moments between Lucy and me aren't uncommon or even uncomfortable. I can wait for her as long as she needs me to. Dad once said that the quiet moments between friends are when the good stuff eventually comes out.

Lucy blinks, and she makes the smallest nod, like she just made up her mind about something. She wipes the tears off her cheeks with both hands and turns to look at me.

"It was about my mother."

Whoa. "What?"

Lucy looks at me with those sad eyes. "When my dad died, we were all in a kind of shock. None of us could believe he was gone because he was such a big part of our lives. And for Mom… she was just so… quiet, like lost at first. She couldn't even go back to work for a little while."

She sighs. "There were days when Mom was so sad that she wouldn't leave her bedroom. She would stay there all day, either sleeping or crying. She wasn't even able to make dinner for us sometimes. Lexi and I would have to stay home from school some days because we didn't want her to be alone like that. Then the principal started asking why we were missing so much school. He knew about our dad, and he was worried about us."

Lucy stops to take a deep breath, which reminds me to do the same. I only know a little bit about the story of Lucy's family from the girl party that night at her house.

"That's when Mom, and I guess me and Lexi, started to have more people to talk to. After our principal called Mom, we started to see more neighbors and friends from school. We didn't live in a very big town, and the other parents would stop by to check in on us regularly, bringing us dinners or just making sure we were okay. Eventually, we all ended up talking to a counselor, someone who could help us with our feelings."

My mind flashes to all the moms sitting on the deck at Lucy's house. *Talking about feelings with others...*

Lucy continued. "Months later, Mom was doing better, and she went back to work. Things slowly started to be more of a new kind of normal. Mom was there for me and Lexi, and we were there for her. We learned how to take care of each other, and over time, some of the pain of the loss we all felt started to be replaced by our love for each other. I mean, that's what the counselor said, and I think she was right. I never told y'all about this because it's something that happened when I was younger. When we moved here, I wanted to bring the memory of Dad with me but leave the sadness in Florida."

"Uh-huh. I get that."

"One day, Mia saw a picture of my dad on my bedside table, and she asked about him. We got to talking, and I shared the story with her that I just shared with you." Lucy takes another breath, and the tears start again. She looks down to her lap and rubs her eyes with both hands. When she looks up at me, I see such pain on her face that I want to jump through my iPad screen to hug her.

"I told Mia our story. It's something that's very personal to me. Something I don't ever want to talk about with anyone other than my best friends—if that. But Mia—" Lucy gulps and starts to choke up, crying harder. "Mia told her older sister, Emma, about my mom, and I guess Emma told some girls at school. It eventually got back to Lexi that some of the girls at school are saying that our mom 'went crazy' when we lived in Florida," she says, making air quotes.

I'm sure that my mouth is hanging open. I feel so useless right now, hearing all this while on FaceTime, only able to just sit there and stare at her. "Lucy, I'm so sorry. I can't believe that Mia would say something like that."

Lucy looks at me, and I see, for the first time ever, a flash of anger. "Well, she did. Lexi is out of her mind about it. She already had it out with Emma right after school today while I was walking home with you. Lexi marched on up to Emma's house and went off right on the front lawn. I guess Mia walked in on the whole thing, and she caught some of Lexi's anger too." Lucy's voice has gotten louder and angrier, but now she looks away as if she's trying to compose herself.

After a moment, I ask, "Did you talk to Mia about it?"

"Not yet. She texted me, saying she was so sorry and all that. And I think she has tried to FaceTime me, like, six times already. I'm just not ready to talk to her right now."

Lucy is rubbing her hands over and around one another, tightly squeezing her fingers together like pretzels. Her cheeks are blotchy red and wet with tears.

"Well, at least she's trying," I say. "Maybe you should talk to her."

Now that I think about it, I realize that while Katie, Mia, and I have known each other since preschool, we've known Lucy for barely a year. After all that pain and sadness, her family got back on their feet and looked out for each other, eventually moving on to a new life with us. But they really only just got here. New town, new school, new friends—that's hard enough before unexpectedly having to relive your past in front of strangers.

"I know Mia, um, let you down, and I'm sorry." I try to find the right words to make Lucy feel better. This hurt between them might affect all of us, and that really bothers me. "This makes me mad at Mia too."

Lucy looks at her hands, and she stops squeezing them together as if she only just noticed what she was doing. Then she looks at me. "I just don't know why Mia would say something like that about my mom—that she was 'crazy.' Mom never went crazy. She was just so sad. We all were."

Lucy sighs. "And that was it. Word got out around school about our dad, our mom, and what we all went through in Florida. The new girls in town—Mom, me, and Lexi—and our secret past."

Lucy has stopped crying. She probably has no tears left. She looks up at me and shrugs as if she's about to say something else.

"Vivian, time for dinner!"

Jeez! I leap off my bed as Dad knocks on my door and walks into my room in one super-intrusive action. He looks at us, oblivious to our conversation. "Oh, hi, Lucy." But as Lucy says a quiet, forced "hi" back, Dad turns to me. "You girls doing okay? Um, dinner will be ready in a few minutes."

"Can I have mine later, Dad?" I ask, trying to tell him with my eyes that this is important.

Dad starts to speak, but his eyes wander over to Lucy on my iPad, and he just says, "Sure, V, no hurry. Just come on down whenever. Bye, Lucy."

Dad closes the door softly behind him, and I listen to his footsteps walking down the stairs. *Score one for Dad on the have-a-clue list.*

I turn to Lucy, who's looking back at me. "Thank you for sharing that. I remember sharing things with you when we were painting together that day, and you made me feel so much better after I was feeling so sad."

Lucy nods and even sort of smiles at me.

I continue, "I know that Mia can sometimes say stuff without thinking, but she wouldn't have done this to be mean to you. I think she was just… stupid about it. We wouldn't be the GirlZ without the four of us, Lucy. I'm sure Mia feels the same way."

Lucy's eyes aren't as red as they were, and the blotchy spots on her cheeks that confused her freckles have faded a bit. She seems a little better as she says, "I know. I mean, I think I know. The hardest part is that I finally feel like this can be home for us. Even in stupid hybrid-school schedules, we're finally happy again—Lexi, Mom, and me. It's almost like how we were together when Dad was still alive. We laugh a lot. We talk about school and just normal things again."

Lucy smiles just a little. "We even make fun of each other and don't take life as seriously as we used to. I have been so glad to have new friends—you, Katie… and Mia. The thought of us not being friends anymore is almost worse than what Mia did. I think that makes me even sadder."

"I know, but it doesn't have to be like that." I hesitate, but I have to ask. "Lucy, do you believe Mia? That she's really sorry?"

Lucy stares right at me through the screen and, after a second, says, "I believe you, Vivian."

* * *

I need to fix this. I can't stand the thought of my best friends not getting along, and the conversation with Lucy dominates my thoughts as I try to eat my dinner. I'm not hungry, so I clear my plate and go grab the leash. It's still light out, and I tell Dad that I'm off to take Buster for a walk.

"Good idea. Buster could use a long walk tonight."

So could I. I don't know what I'm going to say to Mia, but I have to hear her side of the story. It sounds like a big mistake, but on the other hand, Mia *does* occasionally let her mouth get ahead of her brain. It's totally possible she got into gossip mode, and that makes me mad because Lucy's past is nothing to gossip about.

I arrive at Mia's house, and when I ring the doorbell, Emma answers. She looks sad and says quietly, "Hi, Vivian. Um, let me see if I can find Mia."

She hesitates for a brief moment and surprises me by asking, "Did you talk to Lucy today?"

Before I can answer, Mia arrives at the door, dressed in baggy sweats, with her hair up. "Hey, V."

Mia looks down at her feet as if unsure what to do or say next, then Emma quietly turns and walks up the stairs, leaving an awkward silence behind for Mia.

I look at Mia and ask, "Want to come walk with me and Buster?"

"I don't want to take a walk," Mia says, rubbing her eyes. "But you can come into our backyard. Okay?"

Buster and I walk around to the back of the house while Mia disappears inside to put on shoes. I pick up an old tennis ball that's by their deck and keep Buster busy with a game of fetch. Mia walks outside after putting on a pair of ratty old Chuck Taylors and no socks.

"What happened, Mia?"

She avoids my eyes, looking down at the ground. "You mean about Lucy?"

I just look at her, not blinking.

Mia knows the look. She sighs and says, "Lexi has already been by, sounding off on Emma. I don't even know if they're friends anymore."

I let that comment hang there for a second. "Mia, what were you thinking, sharing a story like that about Lucy?"

"I didn't mean for any of this to happen. I *never* said her mom was crazy."

"Well, it sounds like you did."

"I didn't, and it's not my fault the story got turned around the way it did!"

"Oh, come on. Seriously?" I say, my voice rising. "You can't pretend this isn't your fault."

I can feel my face get hot, but before I can say anything else, Buster runs over and puts his paws on my chest. He doesn't like it when I get mad. So I pick up his ball and toss it across the yard. He runs after it so fast that his back paws overtake his front paws, and he barrel-rolls forward, butt over head. I can't help but smile, and Mia even does her little snort laugh.

After a moment, I take a deep breath and sit down next to Mia on the deck, both of us watching Buster chewing on his ball in the corner of the yard. I look over to see that a lonely tear has made a line down the side of her face. It pauses by her chin before finally falling onto her lap.

"I'm sorry. I am sorry, and I don't know what to do," Mia says softly. "Yes, I said something to Emma about Lucy but not in a gossipy way. I promise."

She looks over at me, and I nod back to let her keep going.

"It was more just about… about her, where she came from, that kind of stuff. I guess Emma said something to some girls in her grade, and then the whole thing got twisted around." Mia takes a deep breath as more tears fall. "I just feel horrible."

I put my arm around her and say quietly, "Okay… I totally see how that could happen."

After a long moment, Mia asks, "Did you talk to Katie?"

"No. I came to talk to you. I was sure this was a mistake, and I want to help you fix it. We are all friends after all. I don't want this to… break us up." I kind of fumble the words, but she gets my point, I hope.

Mia shakes her head. "I didn't mean for this to happen. Not at all. I know Lucy has been through so much…"

Her words drift off, replaced by more tears.

"I tried to tell Lucy that, but she won't talk to me. I'm not even sure if there is anything I can say to make this better." She chokes up and looks at me. "Please don't be mad at me too."

"I'm not *mad.*" I turn to face her. "It's just that you need to do more for Lucy. That's why I came here to talk to you. Whatever that *more* is, you need to find it and do it. You need to keep trying until you get through to her. Once you get the chance to say all that, I'm sure she will understand."

Mia looks at me and nods, and I give her a hug. I stay a little longer, sitting next to her on the deck, but there isn't much more to say. Mia has gotten quiet, perhaps thinking about what to do next. I need to get home, so I leash up Buster and walk toward Mia.

"I gotta go." I offer her a smile.

Mia stands up to give me a hug. "Vivian?"

"Yes?"

"Thanks. You're a really good friend." She breaks our embrace to wipe a tear from her

eye. "You're the glue that holds us all together."

We smile at each other and lean in for one more hug.

"It will be okay," I say and walk out the gate toward the street.

On the walk home, I begin to feel a little better. I think Mia will figure this out. I can tell she wants to.

"Good job, Buster buddy," I say as I pat him on the head. Have to hand it to the puppy for easing the tension with the backyard butt flip. But now he's a wet mess, so I do my best to towel him off in the mudroom when we get home.

"There you guys are." Dad bends down to pet Buster and hugs me all at once.

"Hi, Dad."

"That was a long walk. Where did you guys go?"

Dad has this mixture of annoyance and curiosity on his face. I have seen it before, like a half grin below and serious eyes above.

"Mia's house," I say. "We hung out and threw the ball to Buster in her backyard."

"Uh-huh." He says as we walk into the kitchen. It's just us tonight. James is out doing whatever. "Want some milk?"

"Do we have chocolate milk?"

He digs into the pantry and finds the mixture, which he holds up in my direction.

"Yes, please." I sit at the island in the middle of the kitchen.

"So, um, did you ever find out why Mia and Lucy pulled a no-show at ice cream today?" He heaps gobs of chocolate powder into a tall glass.

God. Where do I begin? "Sort of. I guess so."

Dad stops stirring the milk and looks up at me, waiting.

"She and Lucy had kind of a fight…"

Dad goes back to stirring. "Mm-hmm. Syrup swirl on top?"

I smile at him. He gets me.

Dad leans into the fridge to pull out the chocolate sauce. "I wasn't going to say anything, but I could tell Lucy was upset when I saw you guys FaceTiming earlier tonight." He squeezes the syrup bottle and makes big circles on top of the chocolate milk. "Are things better now? With Lucy and Mia?"

My tummy starts to growl. "I don't know. I mean, that's why I went to Mia's house, to try to figure out what to do. Try to help…"

Dad looks up at that and slides the glass over to me. "How's that look? I am a master of the chocolatey swirl."

"Yes, you are." I take a long chocolate-syrupy sip.

A moment passes, then Dad asks, "So, did you girls figure anything out?"

"I hope so. I mean, I was pretty upset that… that they were in a fight, and I wanted to figure out what to do about it. I think Mia is going to keep trying to talk to Lucy until she gets through to her. She just has to tell her she's sorry and make sure Mia knows she means it."

I'm glad I can talk to my dad about this. It all feels so important—today's events really matter to us GirlZ. Maybe I helped out, made things right. I end the story by telling Dad what Mia said to me about being the glue that holds us all together.

"That's a very nice thing of Mia to say to you, honey. She's describing a special friendship quality—loyalty. Yes, there are times when you need to challenge your friends, even tell them you're mad at them. But through all that, you stand by them, which makes you a true friend."

Katie later told me that Mia asked her parents' permission to go see Lucy that night. It was after a bunch of "I'm sorry" texts, but once Mia got to Lucy's house, Mia had much more to say to her, not only about what happened, but also how she felt about Lucy and what she learned because Lucy is her friend.

As I turn out the light by my bed, I'm still thinking about what Dad said—you have to sometimes stand by friends, sometimes defend them, and sometimes even say when you're mad at them. I think I had to do all three today, which is exhausting, but friendships matter. Where would I be without Katie, Mia, and Lucy?

PART II

CHAPTER ELEVEN

DAD

Dinners with Dad, James, and me are still a little strange because we still don't know how to be just the three of us instead of four. The old "How was your day?" line is usually met with the single-word response of "Good," which usually hangs in the air for an uncomfortable length of time.

Tonight, Dad asks, "How was baseball, James?"

"It was okay."

"Just okay?"

"Yeah."

"Why just okay?"

"Just was."

Normally, Dad can probably keep this up long enough to get a full-sentence answer from James, but Dad seems unusually tired tonight. His energy is forced. Just as he is about to ask another question, something catches in his throat, and he starts to cough. Really cough. Like, never-ending.

"Are you okay, Dad?" I ask.

He doesn't look okay. Dad holds up a finger and, with the other hand, holds a napkin to his mouth. After a split second of catching his breath, he starts to cough again then quickly leaves the table to go to the bathroom, trying to settle himself down.

James and I look at each other, and he half shrugs with a blank, noncommittal expression on his face.

When Dad finally gets himself together, he comes back to the table, apologizing for all the noise. "This has been bugging me for the last day or so. Are you guys done with dinner?"

James and I help clear the table as Dad does the dishes. *It's just a cold, right?* I think to myself as I place dirty cups and plates into the sink. I head upstairs to the comfort of my room to FaceTime the GirlZ.

Later, I hear Dad's slippers slipping along the hallway. I yell, "Hi, Dad," and I peek out through my half-open door.

"Hi, V. I'm going to bed early. I need to get some rest."

"Are you feeling any better? Do you think you have a cold?"

"I don't know," he says with a frown and a not-so-convincing shrug. "I'll hug you from over here just to be safe, okay? Love you, honey."

"Love you, too, Dad."

Dad yells, "Good night," to James, who is upstairs in his fully tricked-out attic bedroom. It's like a man cave up there, but smellier. I guess he's turned it into his own me space for the time being. I turn my attention to my book, which is waiting for me with a bag of candy in my fort. There's no one to check on me and tell me it's my bedtime or I need to brush my teeth. I get to read and color as long as I want.

I wake up the next morning still in my fort, still with my clothes on. I peek outside my fort door to see that the sun is barely up as it casts a warm glow through my window. I stretch and roll over, hoping to get a few more hours of sleep, until Dad's voice calling out to James makes me sit up straight. I hear James's footsteps shuffle by my room and turn the corner of the hallway. I rub my eyes and slowly pad over to stand next to James by Dad's bedroom door.

"What's up?" James asks through a yawn.

"I'm not feeling well, guys, and I just spoke with your mom. She is coming over to get you in the next few minutes."

I blink at that. *Mom's coming over? What the…*

Dad goes on, "James, I need you to get some clothes together for you and for Vivian. You're going to stay with Mom for a few days until I feel better. I don't want you to get whatever this is, so please, don't come in here."

"But, Dad…" James looks like he doesn't know what to do. "What are we doing about school?"

Dad doesn't answer, and James starts toward the bedroom door.

"Stop, James," I whisper. "Daddy told you not to go in."

With this, more coughing comes from Dad's room, sounding deep and painful.

James hesitates by the door. "Dad?"

"I don't think you are going to school today, guys. Wait till Mom gets here to figure it out."

I look over at James, who's staring at the door like he's trying to look through it. "Okay, Dad."

I whisper, "What should we do? What's wrong?"

"I don't know, V. We need to get ready for Mom."

We turn around and head toward my bedroom, and James reaches into the hallway closet to get a big beach bag. "Grab your clothes and put them in this bag."

I'm not exactly sure what to take. Usually, Mom or Dad packs things for me if we're going on a trip. I keep a toothbrush, pajamas, and some stuffed animals at Mom's condo. *How long are we going for? What should I bring?*

"James, do you think I need my soccer stuff?"

He looks at me for a moment. "Yes. Bring your soccer stuff, pajamas, and stuff for just hanging around. I'm starting to think we may be there for a few days."

I can hear Dad talking on the phone in a raspy, tired voice. He calls out, "James, Mom is on her way. She should be here in about ten minutes. Take V and wait outside on the front step with your bags, please."

James and I gather the rest of our things, walk downstairs and out the front door, and sit on the steps with our bags. I know about Covid. How can I not? It's all grown-ups ever talk about. It's why we haven't been able to go to school on a normal schedule or see friends like we used to. It's why people started throwing birthday parties (that don't feel like parties) in their cars. Covid is why some of my friends' parents have lost their jobs. My friend Connor wasn't allowed to see his grandmother when she became sick. That sounds like the scariest part of Covid. If you get it, you have to be sick all alone.

I feel James sitting next to me, and I think he even leans into me as we wait for Mom. All I can think about is that Dad and Mom aren't even together anymore, so who is going to take care of him? He's already alone at home, and that makes me sadder than anything else possibly could. I rest my head in my arms to hide the tears falling down my face.

The sound of tires pulling into the driveway breaks into my thoughts, and I look up to see Mom. She steps out of her car, dressed in blue hospital scrubs like she came straight from work. She gives us a caring smile as she walks up to where we're sitting and pulls us in for a big hug.

"I'm going to check on your father now. Why don't you both sit here and wait for me?" Mom starts toward the door and puts on a mask and blue rubber gloves. She stays upstairs for a little while—I'm not sure how long.

"James, what's going to happen to Dad?"

"I don't know. We don't really know what's wrong with him yet. Let's try to not get too worried until we know more."

I know James is trying to make me feel better. Obviously, we've sometimes argued and even fought, especially when Mom and Dad first started not getting along. But James, strangely, has been kind of nice to me lately.

James stands up. "Let's go kick around in the backyard, V. Get your ball out of the garage."

That's when I notice that Buster is making a big fuss in the family-room window. "Uh-oh. Buster looks kind of hyper."

"Get the Buster ball from the garage, and let's play keep-away."

The Buster ball is my old soccer ball from last season. Buster got a hold of it one day when I wasn't home, and he ripped half the side off and put teeth marks all over it. I grab the ball from the pile of outdoor toys stored in our garage and walk around to the back of the house.

Buster runs past James toward me at full speed. Right before he knocks me over, I kick the ball to James, who traps it under his foot then kicks it back to me over Buster's head. Buster practically flips upside down trying to catch it. He's a nice momentary distraction until Mom steps outside.

"Guys… so, Dad is not feeling well, and he has a high fever. I don't like the sound of his cough, and I think he should go to the hospital to be seen by the doctors there. I think he'll be okay, but just to be safe…"

There are sirens in the distance.

We look at Mom, who says, "I don't want you to be freaked out or anything, but an ambulance is on its way, mostly to help get Dad down the stairs. He's pretty weak after such a rough night."

This is surreal. Sirens are always meant for someone else. Fire trucks, ambulances, and police cars speed by to get to other places. Not here. Not to my house. Not for my dad.

This is happening to us? How?

James interrupts my thoughts. "Is Dad going to be okay?"

"Dad has to get tested for Covid before we know for sure, but it's possible that he has it." Mom hugs us again.

She then sits back and tilts her head to the side. I hear it too. There's a commotion in the front yard—loud truck noises, doors slamming, and voices giving orders.

Mom takes hold of our hands and leads us around the house to the front yard. An ambulance is parked on the side of the road by our driveway. A sharp gasping sound makes me jump as it sets its air brakes. A fire truck pulls alongside it, and I'm struck by the pace and urgency of the sudden activity—lights flashing while men and women all walk with purpose and pull boxes of equipment off the truck.

A fireman carrying a radio walks up to Mom to introduce himself. He's wearing this big apron-like thing over his clothing, and he has on a mask and a plastic shield over his face. He looks like he's from outer space. After speaking with Mom for a minute or so, he turns around to give orders to the paramedics. Two of them walk into the house, wearing the same type of masks and aprons and carrying big boxes of equipment.

The fireman then turns to James and me and gets down on a knee to talk to us.

"Hi, you guys. My name is Lou. I'm going to make sure that we take good care of your dad. What are your names?"

"I'm Vivian, and this is my brother, James."

"Well, it's nice to meet you, James and Vivian. You're both very brave—I can tell. So, I guess your dad isn't feeling well?"

"He was coughing a lot last night and this morning," James says.

"Got it. And how about you two? How are you feeling? Do you have a cough or feel achy?"

We say no and that we feel fine.

"That's good to hear. If that changes, make sure you tell your mom, okay?"

All I can do is stare at him.

He goes on. "I want to explain to you how we're going to help your dad. I just sent two paramedics inside to take a look at him and see how he's doing. They're probably going to put a mask on him, and they may also hook him up to oxygen to help him breathe easier. This will make him feel a little better while we move him down the stairs and into the back of the ambulance."

"Can we go with him?" I ask. It's the first clear thought that comes to mind.

"No, Vivian. Not on this ride. We're going to drive very fast to the hospital, so we can get him some medicine as soon as possible to help him feel better. Your mom tells me that she's a doctor at the hospital we're going to, and she'll be able to keep an eye on your dad and see how he's doing every day. But I want you to keep an eye on each other, okay?"

We nod together and say, "Okay." I just then notice that Buster is freaking out in the backyard, barking and jumping around behind the fence.

Lou looks up. "That's a cute dog you have there. What's his name?"

"That's Buster," James says. "I think he's getting a little crazy with all of the noise and the lights."

Lou smiles and opens a Velcro pocket. "Well, I know how to fix that." He shows Buster a big treat shaped like a bone, which makes him sit and whimper. Lou gives Buster the treat and pats him on the head. Firemen think of everything.

Lou's radio on the front of his jacket starts to crackle. He turns his head down to speak into it. "All right. All good here." He looks in the direction of the other firemen and makes a whirly gesture with his hand.

"Okay, guys, we're bringing your dad down the stairs now and putting him into the ambulance. The paramedics tell me that he's doing great. Come on over here to stand with your mom."

His eyes are telling me that he's smiling under his mask, and for a second, I feel like Dad is going to be okay, that these people will take care of him. Lou leads us to the front door, where Mom is standing.

Dad is being taken out of the house in what looks like a metal chair. The firemen then move him onto a stretcher and start toward the ambulance. Lou walks over to Dad and bends down to talk to him, and he nods as Dad answers his questions. Lou waves us over.

"I love you both so much, and I'll be okay," Dad says. His voice is still raspy, and he looks tired.

"I love you, too, Dad," James says. They hold each other's gaze, and James puts his hand on Dad's blanket.

I can't help but cry a little bit. I've never seen my dad look this way. I don't think I've even seen him wear a Band-Aid.

Dad manages a little smile. "I love you, Vivian."

The best I can do is nod a bit as I whimper that I love him too. This has to be just a bad dream. Nothing feels real.

The paramedics move Dad to the waiting ambulance and load him in. Mom, James, and I watch as it pulls out of our driveway, its red lights flashing and the siren kicking in. We don't say anything for a moment. It's just too much for me to take in. Mom holds on to both of us and squeezes my shoulder.

Lou walks up to us and says to come by the fire station sometime to say hello and that we should bring Buster. "Your dad will be fine." His eyes tell me he means it.

It's funny how important people's eyes are now that we're all wearing masks. We're learning how to communicate differently. As we try to be more socially distant, we also try to communicate more often because we miss people. We GirlZ all joke around about "smiling with our eyes" as if we're models, but it's true that you can actually do that. Like my dad's kind eyes. It's like he smiles all the time the way he looks at people—or at least when he looks at me.

Lou and Mom step aside for a few seconds. She nods and thanks him as he turns away to get back into the truck. He waves goodbye as they drive off, no sirens this time. The truck pulls out of sight, and the air becomes immediately still and quiet, like there's an empty hole around us. I was shocked by the noise and action a few minutes ago, but the sudden silence leaves me fidgeting, totally unsure of what to do.

Mom comes over and hugs us.

"I don't get it," James says. "Dad was fine yesterday, and all of a sudden, he just got… I mean, he just started coughing last night and got worse and worse so fast."

Mom looks at him. "I know, honey. That's how this can happen."

"But, Mom," I say, "Dad was always wearing his mask when we went out. He always made sure we had ours on, too, and that we washed our hands. How could this happen?"

Mom nods. "This virus, if that is what he has, can sneak up on people even if they're doing all the right things. We just have to try our best, but sometimes you can still get sick."

We sit down on the front steps. Buster wanders over and leans against me, looking silly with the Buster ball hanging from his mouth, teeth clenched over a loose panel.

That makes me wonder aloud, "Do you think it's from soccer? So many people are around each other at practice and games."

"I don't know, V. It's possible, but I haven't heard about anyone on your team getting sick." Mom hesitates. "Look, guys, there's something that we all need to do. We need to make an appointment to get a Covid test. It's just to make sure we don't have it."

James looks down at his feet and shakes his head. "Getting a stick shoved up my nose doesn't sound like much fun."

Of course, it's not. So many of my friends have had to get tested. Here I was, all year long, hoping I might avoid it.

"Looks like it's our turn." I push my hair back and wrinkle my nose. *Here we go…*

CHAPTER TWELVE

STORM OVER ME

J AMES IS RIGHT—GETTING A STICK shoved up my nose is *not* fun. *Not even close to fun!* Ten seconds of torturous swabbing around each nostril, all in an attempt to get "a sample." *Ick.*

"What kind of sample? Of my brain?" I ask Mom as we sit around the dinner table, reliving the events of the day. "It felt like they were tickling my brain, but not in a silly, tickly way!"

"It does feel like they shove it way up there, doesn't it?" Dr. Mom admits.

Mom says all three of us can stay here instead of moving our things over to her condo. I'm relieved to be in my bed at home, near things that I know. We've been cleaning the house all afternoon. Mom wanted to do most of it, especially in Dad's room. But James and I put on gloves and cleaned the kitchen and all the doorknobs downstairs. It was a lot of work, but it was nice to have something to do. Strange, isn't it? Cleaning and scrubbing actually makes me feel better. Maybe I am getting sick.

The next day is a step in the right direction. Seeing my friends and Ms. Doodle smiling back at me as I log in to remote school lifts my spirits. It's nice to have Mom in the house in the midst of all this. I wonder if she feels the same way.

After school, I decide to spread out my art supplies across the kitchen table and get to work on a new masterpiece. I want to paint a big canvas for Dad with a lot of color to brighten up his hospital room. Just as I finish sketching out a pretty field with birch trees and a big sky, Mom sits down next to me at the table.

Her eyes scan the canvas as I start to apply my greens and blues. "That looks pretty."

"Thanks. If I finish this today, will you be able to bring it to Dad to have in his room at the hospital?"

"That's a great idea, V. He would love that, but I have something to tell you." Mom takes my hand.

I put down my brushes and turn to face her.

"The good news is that our Covid tests came back negative. But for Dad… he tested positive. He has Covid."

I'm looking at Mom but thinking about Dad. "What does that mean? Is he going to be okay?"

"Yes, honey. We think so." Mom nods, like she means what she's saying. "It's only been a few days, but he isn't showing any signs of getting worse. We need to wait and see, but so far, so good. And there is something else. You and James will need to stay home and quarantine for a few days just to be safe."

Ugh, quarantine. More time stuck here in the house with nothing to do. No soccer. No in-school time with my cohort. No playing outdoors with friends. It's back to an at-home lockdown. And what's worse, now Dad is all alone in the hospital, and I can't go visit him.

"For how long?" I abruptly stand up and walk over to the sink.

"About another week, V."

"But why? *We* aren't even sick." I squeeze water through my paintbrushes. My eyes are fixed on the greenish-blue runoff flowing through my hands as I strangle the brushes in frustration. "The test says so. It's just so stupid. The test is the test. It says what it says."

"I know, but we have to be extra careful in case the test is wrong."

On one level I get it, but I'm still just so tired of this whole thing. I spin around from the sink to face Mom, leaving the brushes to rinse on their own. "What? I really don't get how a test like that can be wrong. You're either sick, or you aren't, right? Why can't anything just work the way it's supposed to? Doesn't anything ever just go right anymore?"

My frustration is at its limit, and I can feel it turning into something else within me: rage. A sick-and-tired, enough-is-enough, frustration-fueled rage. Its energy courses through all of my insides—my bones, my stomach, and my lungs. Mom can't see it yet. The negative energy isn't visible, but it's coiling inside me.

Mom continues, "It's just safer if we—"

"That *sucks*, Mom!" The words explode out of me. "I'm *not sick*!"

Mom gasps. "Vivian! You do *not* talk like that to me!"

We may have our arguments, but I never say bad words to Mom. Her shocked expression quickly turns angry. Her eyes lock into that glare that I know means I need to stop. But I'm not going to, and I glare back at her.

My face is hot. My fists balled up tight by my sides, I scream at the top of my lungs, "I *hate* this!"

I turn and run upstairs to my room and slam my door with so much force that a picture frame on my desk falls over and shatters on the floor. But the silence that follows while I'm standing here alone in my room is almost louder than the door slam. A sadness overcomes me as I grip the bedpost at the foot of my bed.

This entire year has been about things being taken away from me. When this whole stupid Covid thing started, I couldn't go to school, see friends, or go on vacation. I couldn't go see my grandparents. I couldn't sit with friends and watch movies together. It's been the year of loss.

I just want to scream, like the rage in me has taken over. I'm scared for Dad. Maybe I'm losing him too. The fear is now mixed with such sadness, anger, frustration, and other emotions that I can't even understand. Tears cover my face and roll down my neck, wetting my T-shirt. It's hard for me to breathe. What is happening to me? I can't get control. *Am I going to die too?*

I start to turn around in place. I don't know why. Maybe I'm looking for something else to hold on to. My mouth is open, but no noise comes out. As my thoughts grip me tighter, I start shaking. I fall to my knees, my hands on my face.

From deep inside, a monster in me takes over, and I scream out a noise that I don't even recognize as my own voice. And it comes out again, louder this time. I'm doubled over on the floor now, sobbing, not knowing what to do or what's happening to me.

Mom runs into the room and drops to the floor. "Vivian. Honey. Oh my God, V… shhh… please. It's okay. Shhh." Mom holds me tightly, trying to settle me down.

Before now, I always thought I was sort of okay, that I could handle it all. But with today's news, all this sadness has just become too much. I lie on Mom's lap while she strokes my hair as I cry uncontrollably. Mom keeps saying that things are okay, that I'm okay. But I'm not okay. This isn't okay. None of it.

"Breathe, Vivian. Clear your head," Mom says as if our shared mantra might work this time.

I try, but no happy thoughts come to me. No pretty colors. Just darkness.

But Mom's voice helps. As I register that she is holding me, my hurried breathing begins to slow. That's a start.

With my eyes closed, I ask, "Why do I feel like this?"

"Vivian… I was hoping you would tell me what you're feeling. Can you describe it to me?"

Having Mom and Dad be apart is something I try not to think about ever. Thinking about having divorced parents only makes me upset, so I try to ignore it, to just forget about it. But how can I possibly do that? I even hate the word *divorce*. It's a mean, sharp-sounding word. Can words really have sharp edges? If I hate the sound of a word, I certainly don't want to talk about it.

Dad going to the hospital in an ambulance keeps playing on the inner reel in my head. Something won't let me stop seeing it, because I miss him. And I'm so scared to lose him.

"Tell me, Vivian. Breathe. You're okay." Mom keeps stroking my hair.

But long before Dad got sick and even before my parents split up, there was always... something else. It was a confused, sad feeling of knowing my parents weren't happy, and it was killing me. I couldn't ignore the quiet tension that permeated our house. It was as if an invisible, mean spirit had moved in and just hung around, lurking.

Almost without knowing, I was always trying to make up for that, to not only force myself to be happy but help Mom and Dad be happy too. I didn't want to cause trouble or give them any reason to be sad or angry or to fight. It was like my job. A job I never felt like I did very well. Like when I lost Buster that day in the woods. I should never have let him run free like that. *If we'd lost him...*

Everything that was familiar to me changed the second Mom and Dad told me they were getting divorced. It's a new home for Mom with another bedroom for me—one that isn't necessarily mine. It means being the three of us but never the four of us. Everything is different now.

"I think it's because I don't know what to do," I say.

"About what, honey?"

I open my eyes and think. "About everything changing for us. About all of us never being together again. I tried… I mean, I wish we could all be happy. I tried to make it so."

Mom flinches. "What? What do you mean, Vivian—'tried to make it so'?"

"I just want so much for all of us to be happy, so I did my best to help with that by trying to be good, but it didn't work. Nothing worked. I can't turn off these sad feelings that are inside me all the time. I want to, Mom, but I just can't." I choke on the last words as tears well up again.

Mom lifts me up with urgency so that I can see her concerned eyes looking at me. "Vivian, I want you to understand something. James, come on in here."

James has been standing outside my door. He walks in with his eyes down, and he looks worried.

"Vivian, honey, your dad and I splitting up has nothing to do with you—or with you, James. Nothing."

Mom is staring at me now with wide, pleading eyes. Eyes that say "This is the truth." Eyes that speak even more clearly than the words she says next. "I don't want you to ever think our divorce is something you caused. It's certainly nothing you could ever fix. Making Dad and me happy is not your job, Vivian. Making *you* happy is your job. Do you understand? Look at me, both of you, and please, hear me." She squeezes my shoulders as if trying to press her words into me.

And that's the hard part. I hear Mom's words. I'm sure they make sense, but they don't make me feel less sad or defeated. I close my eyes as she pulls me into her, hugging me tightly. James kneels next to me and puts his hand on my shoulder. He doesn't say anything, but I know he's there, close to me.

Mom goes on. "And yes, Vivian, the feelings you're having about Dad and me must be very sad and even scary. But they're normal feelings, honey. There's nothing wrong with feeling the way you do. Sad, confused, and even angry. That's okay and, well, very much like most kids would feel—should feel. They're feelings that you have to accept—I mean, to face them and let them be, because that's the only way to eventually let them go when it's time."

"When is that? When do I let them go?" I ask.

"When you make peace with your feelings. When you're able to know they're there and that it's okay to feel the way you do and when you're able to talk about them with me, Dad, or even your friends. Do you understand what I mean when I say that?"

"I think so." Yes, I do think so.

"This isn't about you, Vivian, James. The number one thing Dad and I totally agree on is that the two of you are the brightest lights in our lives. You both are the source of our happiness, always."

Her words begin to sink in as Mom holds me and James for I don't know how long. Slowly, the scary thoughts begin to quiet and feel further away as sleepiness takes over. Mom puts me in bed and stays with me until I begin to drift away.

"I love you, Vivian," Mom whispers in my ear. "Dad and I love you. Nothing will ever change that. Nothing," she repeats over and over.

Mom's words make the storm in my mind begin to fade. Darkness takes its place, but it's like a blanket that quiets me. I imagine stars all around, thousands of little specks of light coming through.

CHAPTER THIRTEEN

FRIEND THERAPY

As I wake up the next morning, I feel rested, maybe even refreshed. Except for one thing—James is sitting on my bed, looking at me, which is weird.

"Hi, V."

"Hi, James. Um, why are you sitting on my bed?"

"It's almost ten o'clock. Mom wants me to get you up for breakfast, and you were sound asleep. I had to shake your foot a few times."

"Okay. Thanks." I yawn and stretch my arms. "I'll be down in a minute."

James stands up and heads to the door, but he stops and looks at me for a second.

"Are you… okay?"

After last night's events, it's a fair question, one I'm sure to get from Mom when I get downstairs. I think I'm okay, and I realize that I'm seriously hungry. I guess having a freak-out can take a lot out of you. I want a doughnut.

"I want a doughnut."

James half smiles at me. Then he leaves and closes the door behind him. I hear the stairs creak as he makes his way to the comfort of his attic room. He never really thanked me for that, come to think of it.

Time for my fuzzy bathrobe and some breakfast. As I step off the landing of the stairs and turn the corner into the kitchen, I see a tired-looking Mom sitting there at the island, drinking her coffee, probably not her first cup. She stands up to give me a big, long hug. Hugs always feel better in a warm bathrobe.

"Want some breakfast?"

"I want a doughnut."

"I don't think we have any doughnuts. How about a waffle?"

I always like waffles with tons of butter and syrup in the morning. Sometimes Mom lets me put Nutella on them. "With Nutella?"

Mom laughs a little, slides the frozen waffles into the toaster oven, and sets the Nutella jar on the table. "You look kind of tired."

"So do you."

"I am. I stayed up late last night after you went to bed. That was quite a moment we had, wasn't it?"

Here we go...

"I think I'm okay now, Mom. I feel a little better."

Mom's eyes are studying me. She knows me too well. "Are you telling me the truth or just avoiding the subject?" Mom has the eyebrow up, and I'm not sure if she believes me.

I take a sip of OJ as I think about what to say next. Of course, I want to avoid the subject, but I'm sure Mom won't let it go if she thinks I'm faking. Maybe I am still upset somewhere inside, but I don't feel like a big rock is squeezing the air out of me, like I did last night. I tell Mom this.

"A big rock? That's a good way to describe it. It's like saying you feel a lot of pressure."

"I prefer 'big rock,'" I say through my mouthful of Nutella-soaked waffle. This gets a nod from Mom, along with a smile. She's satisfied for the moment.

I put away my dishes, and Mom gives me another hug. She takes a step back with her hands on my shoulders. "I love you, V. You're a great kid."

"I love you, too, Mom."

When I get back upstairs, my iPad dings. It's Katie on FaceTime. "Hi!" she says brightly. "Um, I think you have Nutella or something on your bathrobe."

Katie is all dressed for soccer, with her usual game-day pigtails—a Katie thing. Seeing her dressed in our team uniform stings just a little. It's a reminder that I'm sitting around in quarantine instead of playing today. But as usual, Katie is smiling at me, and her smile looks even bigger when she's in pigtails because there's more of her face to look at. Katie being here, even on an iPad, brightens my day.

"Yeah, I just had waffles and Nutella with Mom."

I grab a tissue to try to wipe away the Nutella. That just makes it worse, resulting in more of a blob-like mess.

Katie laughs. "Now it just looks like poop."

That gets me laughing too—a long, silly giggle fit. After last night, I'm glad to know that laughter is still inside me.

Once she settles down, Katie wipes the giggle-induced tears from her eyes. "What are you going to do today? Can you go outside or anything?"

"I'm not sure. Maybe Mom will let me take Buster for a walk around the pond or something," I say weakly. *How lame is that?* The highlight of my day is taking the dog for a walk around the pond.

But Katie's eyes go wide. "Hey, maybe I can come by later and say hi from the driveway or something!"

"That would be awesome. Can you ask your mom?"

"I'll do that and text you."

"Good luck in the game today," I say. "I'm bummed not to be there."

Katie practically cuts me off midsentence. "You'll be there next week, right? Don't worry—there's still a lot of soccer to play this season. It's only one game. We need you back soon, so just do the quarantine thing, and then you'll be back out there again. Easy peasy."

"Thanks, Katie. Maybe see you later, I hope."

A few minutes later, Mom walks into my room, still holding her favorite coffee mug she likes to use on weekends. It says, "Patience is my superpower." It's supposed to be funny. So sometimes we'll laugh about our superpowers as a family. Like, James's superpower is to annoy me more than anyone in the universe, or Dad's superpower is having a Zoom voice loud enough to knock down buildings with a single sentence.

"Hey, V." She flattens out the corner of my bed and sits down. "Who was that?"

"Katie. Getting ready for soccer today." My eyes wander down to her coffee mug. "Mom, I want a superpower."

"Really? That sounds fun." She looks at me for a second. "If you could have any superpower in the world, what would it be?"

That's an easy one. "I wish it would be something like Wanda Maximoff's power in the Avengers movies. That would be awesome."

"Wanda. Hmm. Yes, nobody wants to mess with her." Mom smiles and looks at her mug. "I actually meant superpowers, here on earth—"

"Mom, Wanda does live on earth." *I mean, duh.*

"I know. I know, but I mean for us non-superheroes, I think superpowers can actually be real. We just need to look for them or at least know when we see them."

Hmm. Not entirely helpful, but maybe she has a point. I think out loud, "But what about the GirlZ? We should make up cool nicknames for each other that only we know about."

Mom laughs. "I like that idea. In fact, I think you GirlZ are pretty special and that, yes, you each may have superpowers…" Mom looks at me. "Okay, who do you want to start with?"

I roll over and face the other side of my room as Mom waits for my answer. "Katie."

"Ah, yes," Mom says. "Katie has all kinds of powers. Like super speed, like the Flash."

I smile a little bit. I don't do DC heroes, but Mom wouldn't get that. "Yeah. The Flash is cool, but…" I think about the FaceTime I just had with Katie. "Katie is always so positive. She has a way of seeing the bright side of everything and helps others around her see the same."

Mom nods, but she doesn't say anything as she waits for me to go on. A picture forms in my mind—Katie in a superhero costume, spreading an almost-magical bright light all around her. Dark forces can't get to her or anyone around her.

"She's the Lightkeeper," I say to Mom.

"I like that name. Um, because of her always seeing the bright side of things?"

"Yes, but even more so that she can make things better at the right time, like she did just now."

Mom nods as she takes a sip of coffee. "That's a good one. Who's next?"

I start to think about Lucy. A few weeks ago, she came over to paint outside on the deck. When Lucy and I paint together, we usually don't talk a lot. Unlike with my other friends, it's totally fine. "Lucy."

"Lucy," Mom answers. "She's so sweet. I can't wait to hear this one."

I don't know if I should tell Mom this part, especially after last night, so I stay quiet for a minute.

"What?" Mom asks, looking at me. She starts to rub my foot.

"One day, I talked to Lucy about… us. About how I was feeling." I pause for a second and look up at Mom. Her expression doesn't change. In fact, I think she smiled a little bit. "Lucy put her brush down and listened, not saying a word. She always makes me feel like it's okay to talk to her about anything."

"Mm-hmm." Mom gives me an encouraging look. "I think Lucy is different. Good different."

"Yes!" That's it. "She's quiet but in a good way. Like, I can talk to her, and she will just listen, not judge. She has, like, this quiet spirit that makes me feel like I can tell her anything."

"Ah, a quiet spirit. That sounds like a superpower right there. What do you call it?"

I think about that for a moment. Lucy's quiet spirit has the power to calm me down and chase away the darkness of my scary thoughts. I guess that's a super-power too.

I look up at Mom. "She's like a… She's the Spirit Whisperer."

"Ooh, now that's pretty cool." Mom smiles. "Very cool, actually. Okay, one more."

"Mia… She's just crazy funny."

"Yes, I know. Is being funny a superpower, though?"

"No, I don't mean it that way. She is funny, but… Katie's positive light and Lucy's quiet spirit gently make things better, but Mia just crashes into a bad day and forcefully elbows it out the door."

Mom laughs. "Sounds just like her mother."

I go on. "And she's very protective of us GirlZ. She always steps in if something goes wrong with one of us."

I think back to the day we lost Buster in the woods when she said to me, so matter-of-fact, *"Oh, I had it under control. I was going to say it was all my fault. That*

I'm the one who let Buster off leash, and then he ran off. I wouldn't let anything bad ever happen to you."

I wouldn't have let Mia take all the blame for that, but the fact she was willing to do so, well… "Mia's the Protector."

"The Protector," Mom says. "Yes, I like that too. She's a tough one, that girl. I certainly wouldn't want to mess with her."

We laugh at that, then she looks at me. "So… what about you, Vivian? Any ideas on your superpower?" There goes Mom's eyebrow again—right up.

The fact is, I have no clue. "I never really stopped and thought about it until now. What do you think?"

Mom looks at me for a second and stands up from the bed. She leans over to kiss my forehead. "Well, I know you have one in there, honey." Her hand cups my face. "But I think that's something you have to discover on your own."

She turns to leave my room then stops to give me a big, warm smile. I was hoping for a little more help than that, but she's probably—maddeningly—right.

* * *

The rest of the day is boring. Really boring. I wish I was at that game, standing in goal for my soccer sisters. Mom, James, and I take Buster for a walk around the pond and through the trail in the woods. James is going on forever to Mom about some baseball game, so I walk on ahead, alone with Buster and my thoughts.

I can't stop thinking about Dad, of course. But I don't want to bring it up. We talked enough about it last night. Mom told me that she speaks with his doctors every day and he's doing okay. I decide to leave it at that and try to think about other things. I wonder how many goals Katie scored in the game today.

A lazy walk around the pond turns into a lazy hang-out in our backyard. It's almost four o'clock, and I still haven't heard from Katie, which is weird. I don't know how the game went, and she hasn't called about coming by later. Maybe she just forgot about me.

"Mom, have you heard from Katie's mom about her coming by later today?"

She hasn't. So I close my book and head upstairs to see if there are any messages on my iPad. Just as I get to the top of the stairs, I hear a loud honk from the front of the house. There are sounds of car doors opening and closing mixed with voices.

Then I hear Mom's footsteps walking through the house out to the porch. "Well, hello there, girls."

"Hi, Dr. Hopewell!"

What? It sounds like the GirlZ are out there. Laughter is mixed with some sort of commotion on the front lawn.

"Um, V, you might want to come downstairs and see this!" Mom yells up to me.

I turn and run down the stairs two steps at a time before jumping onto the landing. As I hurry out the door to join Mom on the porch, she looks at me, eyes wide, with a big smile on her face. She tilts her head in the direction of our front yard.

And there they are, the GirlZ, standing in our drive-way with big grins on their faces, smiling and laughing.

I blink twice to make sure it's real. Amazingly, Lucy and Mia are standing next to each other. Lucy's arm is around Mia's shoulder in a silly half hug, half squeeze.

Look at them, happy and together again! I wonder for a split second if that's what this is all about. Like, they came by to show me that things are okay between them and they're friends again.

But then something else up my street catches my eye. There's a burst of color and noise as all my soccer sisters pedal toward me on their bikes. Mel is in front, waving. As they roll up to my front lawn, I notice they are all still wearing their game uniforms. I put my hands to my face and begin to laugh. There is enough happiness inside me to light up the sky.

"Hey, V!" Mel yells. "We missed you today!"

Before I can respond, Lucy's mom leans on the horn of her big truck. It's parked in our driveway with both doors open and Lexi in the front.

"Hi, Vivian!" Dr. G yells from the driver's side. "Hope y'all are ready to party!"

"What are you all up to?" Mom yells back.

Katie says, "We know you're stuck at home, V, so we brought a dance party to you!"

Lexi, Mel, and my soccer sisters start tying balloons to the fence posts, and then Lucy's mom cranks up the truck's stereo. Then everyone starts jumping around and dancing in our yard.

"Excuse me, but we're in quarantine, Doctor!" Mom laughingly yells out to Dr. G, who doesn't really seem to care.

"We know that! So y'all just stay up there on your front porch, and we'll be fine down here! It's like you're on stage. Now, get with it!"

I jump and dance all around the porch. Mia is showing off her fancy moves, and we all do the same. The GirlZ are pointing at me and singing—sort of yelling—in unison to every song, like they're serenading me. It's all our favorite music that we like to listen to, as if they made a playlist just for the occasion.

It's impossible for the neighbors not to hear all the noise, and some come out to watch. They all know about Dad and what we've gone through lately, so they smile and wave. The dance party lasts for almost an hour. I haven't really seen anyone in person for almost a week, and there they are, my three best friends in the world and my entire soccer team, dancing around the front yard just for me. It really is a party and maybe the most fun I've had all year.

We are all breathless as the music quiets down. Lucy and her mom heave a huge gift basket with flowers, wine, and all my favorite snacks over and set it by our front steps, which makes Mom all mushy.

Then Mel leads the chant. "One. Two. Three. We love you, Vivian!"

And I love them too. Last night was terrible. The entire year feels like it's been terrible. But tonight, all of my friends are here to help me forget about all that.

"We get to see you from *only* six feet away next week, right, V?" Katie asks from the front lawn.

"That's right, girls," Mom says. "Just a few more days, and Vivian can be down there dancing with you."

Katie smiles at me. "Sorry I never called you today. I had some planning to do after the game." That means this was all her, which is amazing. "Oh yeah, I almost forgot—we won!"

Mom and Dr. G air-hug and blow kisses at each other. The GirlZ and I do the same as they're getting ready to leave, and we layer on the drama, which makes the moms laugh.

Then Mom and I head inside to attack the gift basket, in search of snacks. I've come so far since the low point of last night. Everyone should have a best friend to pick them up when they're down. I am so lucky to have three of them.

CHAPTER FOURTEEN

GROWN-UPS

Mom arrives home from work today, looking like she just ran out of the hospital and was being chased. She's a hot mess. As she steps out of the car in her blue hospital scrubs and white coat, I see that her hair is up in an unusually messy ponytail with a pencil stuck through it. She's trying to manage her phone while holding a coffee and fumbling with something in her purse. Almost in slow motion, the purse tips out of her hand and falls on the driveway, spilling ChapStick, a phone charger, a notebook, and pens everywhere. Epic fail.

Mom fires off a bad word in the direction of her purse... a real nasty one too.

I've been sitting on the porch with my sketchbook, and I feel like I've suddenly been transported to the front row of a movie theater, watching a hilarious comedy. Mom is so good at keeping it together most of the time that it drives me a little crazy. So to see her all futzed, picking up the contents of her purse while trying unsuccessfully to text and balance a coffee with one hand, is almost like seeing a unicorn dancing in my driveway. If only I had my phone, I could narrate the whole thing and become an instant TikTok sensation.

Mom walks up the driveway and looks up at me as if just noticing that I've been sitting here the whole time, watching her flail about. She offers a little smile, but before she can say hello, her phone dings. I'm pretty sure I hear her say another bad word under her breath.

Mom sits down next to me on the steps, exhaling, and makes kind of a… well, an old-man noise, like, exhaustion mixed with achy joints. Usually, that's exactly what it is.

"Hi, V." She takes a long sip of coffee. "Not my finest moment."

"You just made an old-man noise."

Mom's expression freezes for a split second as her eyes come to rest on the front lawn. Her lips curl into a little smile. "Yes, don't tell anybody. Work has been just nonstop lately, and I think it's making me old."

We both laugh at that. I ask, "What's with the pencil?"

"Huh?"

"In your hair. You have a pencil stuck in your ponytail." I point up at the top of Mom's head, and her hand absentmindedly follows the direction of my playful gaze.

"Oh, I do that sometimes when I'm juggling things at work. I forgot that was in there. It's kind of like having an extra pocket."

I laugh, and after a brief second, she does too. We sit for a while as I make a few changes to my drawing, and Mom sets her phone to silent so she can have some quiet time. "Just for a few minutes," she says. "I want to enjoy some fresh air on the porch. Haven't been outside all day."

I look at Mom and notice that she is chilling out a bit now. In fact, her smile hasn't totally faded yet. She seems lost in thought about something nice, or maybe the fresh air is doing its thing.

"When did you know that you wanted to be a doctor?" I ask.

One hand lowers the coffee, and the other takes the pencil out of her hair. "Well, I remember knowing in high school that I wanted to study all I could about medicine. I just always enjoyed the science behind it— the chemistry of medicine, the biology of things—and I like the idea of applying it all to help people feel better when they're sick."

Mom looks out at the yard and takes a sip of her supersized coffee. I can't help but notice. "That coffee is bigger than your head."

"Ha. Yes, this was a day for an extra dose of caffeine." She takes another long sip.

She hasn't mentioned it yet, so I ask, "Did you visit Dad today?"

Mom's phone lights up with a message. She takes a quick peek and turns it screen-side down on the porch. She nods. "Yes, honey, I did. In fact, that was how I ended my rounds today. He was the last patient I saw."

That's a weird thing to say. "Wait. Dad's *your* patient?"

"No, honey. Sorry, just a figure of speech. He has other doctors still looking after him." Mom's staring at our yard, but her eyes look like they're seeing something else that's very far away.

"Um… is it okay that I ask you about him?"

Mom's slumped shoulders straighten up, and she lowers the coffee cup from her mouth. She seems a little startled. "Oh. Yes, of course, V. You can always ask about Dad."

I'm glad to hear that, but I sit there quietly, unsure what to say next.

After a beat, Mom says, "I can see why you asked that. Yes, I do see Daddy and am happy to talk to you about how he's doing. Sorry. I'm just super tired. I guess my mind is a little bit elsewhere at the moment."

"Mom…"

I'm bending the corner of my sketchbook up and down while looking at my feet. She puts a hand on my arm, waiting for me to continue. I'm just not sure if I should. A thought, more like a question, has been rolling around in my mind these last few weeks. I'm just not sure how it will go over if I ask. But really, Mom is the only one who can answer it.

Here goes…

"Was it your work… how busy you always are… that made you and Dad argue all the time?"

I watch Mom's face, and interestingly, she just stares at me, not moving a bit. Blank. The moment goes by slowly as Mom holds my gaze. Then she surprises me with a little smile, and her expression slowly changes. It's a subtle uplift of her facial features, like the sun rising inch by inch. "That is a very good question, Vivian. A very good, very fair question for you to ask me."

Well, at least she's still smiling.

Mom takes another long sip of coffee then looks at me. "I think your dad and I thought work was what we would argue about, but actually, it wasn't exactly that."

"Then what?"

Mom nods. "There are a few things that your dad and I were trying to deal with, and, yes, work was one of them. But it wasn't just my work so much. It was both of our jobs and how they're very different now versus what they used to be before the pandemic."

Mom hesitates for a second. "I have been very busy this year, Vivian. Busier than I ever thought I could possibly be. There are so many sick people in the world at the moment. And your dad's job has changed too. Working from home means that he doesn't get to be around his friends and coworkers anymore, and that's really uncomfortable for him. He's used to being around people, not stuck at home in front of a Zoom screen.

"These are both unexpected changes we've had to learn to deal with this year, mostly on our own." Mom continues, "But maybe that wasn't the right way to go about it. Maybe we needed to talk about it more—have it all out in the open with one another instead of keeping it inside. In fact, your dad and I talked a little bit about this just today."

I sit up at that. I don't really know what to say, so I look at Mom and wait.

"Yes," she says. "Just today."

She looks over at me, and her eyes all of a sudden look brighter, the edges of her mouth still curled upward.

"What do you mean?" I ask.

"Well, when I visited Dad this afternoon, I was able to spend a few minutes alone with him after the other doctors had left." She pauses and looks at her hands. "We both said some things to each other that I think cleared up some… some misunderstandings."

"Like what?" *We've never talked like this before.*

"Sort of out of the blue, your dad said that he has always been very proud of me being a doctor, and he hopes that I never forget that." Mom's smile grows. "He just kind of said it, and I've been thinking on the drive home how I really needed to hear that from him. I guess that opened up a bit of a conversation that maybe we should have had a while ago." Mom turns her head to look at me. "Does this make sense to you?"

"Sort of, I guess. I mean, I know that you and Dad acted differently with each other this year."

Mom puts her arm around me as I lean into her. "You're right, Vivian. Yes, and I think today Dad and I may have put a few of the pieces together as to why that is. We haven't talked with each other that way in a while."

We sit quietly together. Mom is looking off at something, or maybe nothing, out over the front lawn. I think, in her mind, she may be back at the hospital with Dad. *I wonder if…*

"Mom, do you think you and Dad will talk about it more?" I hear the hope in my voice.

Mom holds me a little tighter. She's still looking out across the lawn, not blinking, not moving. "Vivian. That's a very good question."

CHAPTER FIFTEEN

NEWS

I'VE BEEN LYING IN BED all afternoon, super bored, and I'm antsy. My conversation with Mom yesterday is still rolling around in my brain. I feel like something has changed, but I'm not entirely sure what. Mom had to get upstairs to return what she said were probably a zillion phone calls before I could ask more about her and Dad.

I need to get out of the house to try to figure this out. A bike ride is definitely in order, so I dig around in my bureau for my awesome Avengers hoodie, but it's nowhere to be found. I think it's in the mudroom, so I run downstairs and crash right into Mom just as she was bringing a pile of laundry upstairs.

"Oops!"

"Careful there, V. Where are you off to?"

"I'm going on a bike ride."

"That sounds good. Where are you going?"

"I don't know. Just around."

Mom stops halfway up the stairs and looks at me. "That's fine, but be back before five to wash up for dinner, okay?"

"Okay. Do you have my hoodie in there? The Avengers one?" I point with my chin at the pile of laundry in her arms.

"Actually, yes I do." Mom digs midway into the pile and throws my hoodie to me, more like at me, and it sails over my head into the hallway.

I roll my eyes. "Nice throw, Mom."

When I bend down to pick up my hoodie, a cardboard box tucked away in the corner catches my eye. I look into it to find a bunch of old pictures, books, and other things that look like they are about to be thrown away or put into storage. I set my hoodie aside and begin to dig around. Down at the bottom of the box, I find the picture of Mom and Dad the night they met. Who would want to store this away? It would always sit in plain sight because the story behind it was so special. It tells a story about the beginning of them, of all of us. I look over my shoulder to make sure nobody is around, and I tuck the picture under my hoodie. This picture isn't getting put into some storage box—no way.

I head out to the garage and get on my bike. I really don't know where I'm going to ride to, and I guess that's fine with me. My mind drifts back to what Mom said yesterday about her conversation with Dad. She was even smiling when she talked about him. That never happens, at least not that I can remember.

Bike rides always make me happy. I don't even need to go anywhere in particular. In fact, that's kind of the point today. I just need to do something, and if I can't be somewhere else or with someone, I might as well be my own best friend for the moment. Besides, the sun feels nice, and the blue sky makes everything else look more pretty, warming my thoughts and helping me think through everything.

When I get back home, Mom and James are sitting on the porch. Buster comes running around the house to greet me, shaking his tail so hard that his butt swings from side to side and he looks like he's about to tip over.

"Hey, Buster, buddy, buddy," I say in my puppy voice as I give him a hug. Buster is always excited, no matter what, but he really gets excited when I come home from wherever. Dad likes to call him Mr. Wigglebutt when he gets like that.

"Hi, Vivian. I was wondering when you'd be back." Mom's looking at me with a little smile on her face. "I have some good news for you. Have a seat."

I take off my helmet and sit down next to Mom. She looks at me, and so does James with a goofy grin on his face.

"What?" I ask. *This is weird.*

"Daddy is coming home from the hospital tomorrow," Mom says as she puts her arm around me.

That's not at all what I expected. James smiles at me, nodding. Mom looks at me, waiting for me to say something.

"Really?" It's all I can say. *Did I just hear that right?*

Mom gives me a big squeeze. "Yes, honey. Dad has gotten much better, and the doctors say he can come home to rest up as he continues to get back on his feet.

He'll need to sleep a lot, and we need to stay away from him for a few days just to be safe. But it's good news, V. He's ready to come home. The doctors say he's almost all better. He just needs to rest, which he can do here at home instead of in the hospital."

I hug Mom, and James leans in too. We sit there for a full minute just like that. Then something occurs to me. "How are we going to take care of Dad? Are we going to get a nanny or something?"

James smiles even bigger at that. He looks at me then at Mom.

Mom says, "No, Vivian. I'm going to stay here for a little while to help out Dad."

I just look at Mom, stunned, mouth open as her words replay in my mind, assuring me that I heard her right.

She pats James on this hand. "James said that I can stay in his old room." Mom turns to face me and puts a hand on my shoulder. "But listen, it's just for a couple of weeks while we get Dad back on his feet."

Dad's coming home. He's going to be okay. Mom is going to stay with us, all of us together again.

My mouth is still open.

"It's just for a little while, V, like a week or two." Mom says again. "Do you understand what that means?"

I look at her and say, "Yes," which maybe is true. Maybe it's not, but at the moment, I am too happy to care.

So, we take the afternoon to organize Dad's room to make it cozy for him, bringing in extra pillows and blankets so that he can sit up in bed when he wants to.

Mom also put a few books on his bedside table, the ones he got for his birthday but hasn't had a chance to read. It looks like he'll have plenty of time to read now.

As I'm folding sheets, my eyes wander over to the bookshelf on the wall. There is an old picture of Dad from when he was in the Marines, standing in front of a bunch of other soldiers in a faraway place. He looks super skinny, and I'm always struck by the fact that he isn't smiling. In the many other pictures around our house, Dad is always smiling or even laughing, but not in this one. The thought occurs to me that I would rather see something happy live in that space. *In fact...*

I have an idea—a master plan, actually.

That's what needs to be in that room! On that bookshelf. Something happy! Something to make them remember... them.

I drop the sheets on the bed and run downstairs to the mudroom. I dig into my cubby to retrieve the picture of the night Mom and Dad met. I stare at it for a long second as I think about how I can pull this off.

Mom is folding towels by the laundry, so I hide the picture behind my back and scoot by her then run up the stairs. I want this picture to be noticed, so I move the books around on the shelf to make an open space in the middle.

Perfect, right in plain sight. Now, I just need Mom to see it.

"Hey, honey."

I jump, startled, as Mom walks into the room. She puts the fresh towels down at the foot of the bed and looks around the room. "Nice job in here. You made it very cozy."

"Yup, totally." I pick up the towels and place them on a chair near the bookshelf. Time to put Operation Memory Lane into action. I turn around to face Mom. The picture is right behind me, just over my shoulder. "You think he'll like it?"

"Of course, he will," she says. "Dad can't wait to be home. He really misses you guys, this house."

"Mm-hmm," I say. "Um, do you think he will want to read? I mean books? There are a lot in here." I turn my head toward the bookshelf. *Come on. See the picture!*

"Oh, um, probably," Mom says. "I mean, he will get to that after he rests up for a few days. I like that stack you put by his bedside table."

Shoot. Not the bedside table. Look over here…

Mom smiles and turns to leave.

Oh no! I have to think of something quick. I reach over to the bookshelf, grab the largest book I can find, and tip it over. It falls to the floor with an extra-loud *thud*. "Oops!"

That gets Mom's attention.

"My bad," I say as I bend over to pick up the book. I hold it up to her. "Mom, is this yours?"

She steps across the room to have a look. "Yes, but I haven't read it in, like, forever."

Mom leans over me to put it back in its place on the shelf. I turn with her and stare at the picture of her and Dad. Mom is behind me, looking over my shoulder.

"I remember that night," she says quietly. "That's when we met."

Got her.

I reach up and hand the picture to her, but she doesn't take it. Instead, she holds one side of the frame, and I hold the other, as we stand close to one another.

"Is it true you never saw him again after that night?" I ask. "I mean, until you moved here to Boston?"

"Yes. In fact, I never thought I would ever see him again. He was just driving through DC with his friends on a road trip, and he left the day after. This picture was taken at the end of the night after we'd been talking and laughing and having so much fun getting to know each other. I just... I mean, it was a lot different back then, with no cell phones or social media. Easier to lose touch with people, so I thought that was that."

I want Mom to relive the rest of the story. Something about standing in this room with her, knowing that Dad is coming home tomorrow, makes me think this is my chance to get her to remember him—to remember *them*. That they were happy once.

I ask, "Can you tell me how he found you?"

We sit down on the bed together.

"Well, he didn't exactly 'find' me. It's more like..."

"What?" I ask, looking up at her.

She smiles and says, "It's sort of strange to say now, so many years later, but I guess that I—I mean, we— always felt like fate brought us back together because the whole thing was so... unexpected."

"Why unexpected?" I lean into her lap.

Mom starts to stroke my hair. "I moved to Boston for my first job after I finished medical school. I didn't know anyone at the time, and that was fine with me. All

I did was work anyway. But one day, I was sitting at my favorite café, having breakfast, and this loud group of people was sitting near me."

She pauses for a moment, sitting with the memory before going on. "It was pretty annoying because the café was usually a nice quiet place to sit, drink coffee, read, or just relax. But they were talking loudly about something that happened the night before, just laughing it up and disturbing the whole place. Pretty rude, come to think of it. But through all the noise, I kept on hearing this one laugh from the group, one that I recognized but couldn't figure out how.

"Then one of the girls in the group—the loudest one, actually—excused herself from the table, and that's when I looked over. Sitting there facing me was your dad, and you should have seen the way he looked at me... I think it took his boy brain a few seconds to put it together, but he recognized me, and I recognized him. He sort of waved at me and then came over to my table to introduce himself—or reintroduce himself, I guess. Of course, I remembered him because I don't think I've ever laughed so hard as that night I first met him. Even after so many years, that's something I hadn't forgotten."

Mom's eyes leave the photo, and she looks over at me. "In fact, that was more than four years after this picture was taken. I was all alone in a brand-new city, and there he was. That boy from the restaurant."

Mom looks across the room, but her eyes say she's somewhere else entirely. After a moment, she turns to me and smiles. "What are the odds of that?"

Even though I've often asked myself the same question, wondering about the magic of it all, I still don't have an answer. Except maybe fate.

"I don't know," I say softly. "It's amazing, actually."

A long, quiet moment passes by as we sit there together.

Mom is still holding the picture, studying it. "Yes. Yes, it is," she says softly.

She kisses me on the head, stands up, and puts the picture back on the shelf. After adjusting it to the center, she takes one last look. As she turns around, she smiles at me. "Come on, V. Help me with these sheets."

We fold in silence, standing next to each other, and make the last few cozy adjustments. I'm smiling on the inside as Mom and I pause at the door to take one more look around at the room.

When Mom goes out to the grocery store, I run up to my room to FaceTime with the GirlZ to tell them Dad's coming home.

"That's amazing!" Katie says.

The GirlZ pepper me with questions:

"When can we come visit?"

"When is he going to coach again?"

"Can we help bring anything over?"

Mom already told all the parents, and Mia says her mom is cooking up, like, a week's worth of meals for us. That's exciting because Mrs. Gallo is an amazing cook, and so is Mia. I'll have to tell Mom to make sure there's room in the fridge.

In fact, there's still a lot to do to get ready for Dad's homecoming. But it's not enough to keep me from day-dreaming about what it all may mean.

CHAPTER SIXTEEN

HOMECOMING

MY OWN FIRST TRIP TO the hospital, back when I was little, was really unexpected, and it was messy. James and I were playing with our friends up at the pond. We had this game where we would throw rocks at bugs on the water, always trying to find the biggest rocks to make the biggest splashes. This was a favorite game of ours on quiet, lazy summer evenings. The parents would sit outside on the deck, talking like they always do, and we kids would disappear to make up our own fun.

There's something different about summer nights with friends compared to other seasons. We can be free to do anything. We don't need to waste time putting on coats like in the cold months. We probably don't even need shoes and definitely not socks. The warm air and the late-setting sun give us more time to play. Even parents are more relaxed, not hovering as much.

It's hard to explain, but I feel an energy from nights like that. If I stop for a second, I can hear the noises of outdoor life—bugs, birds, and frogs, all singing to each other. It's like they get to go out and play at night too. Even the smell of the forest in summertime is noticeable. Mom would say our smell was noticeable, too, when we would come home all sweaty and dirty from chasing each other in games we would make up each night.

Splash!

James threw a huge rock that hit the water like thunder. We watched the ripples spread outward and across the shallow section we were standing in. They moved slowly across the pond, over stumps sticking out from the bottom, and to the other shore.

Something by my feet caught my eye, and I bent over to get a closer look. There was the tip of a rock sticking out of the mud, and it looked like a good one. As I dug my fingers into the wet, gooey muck, I realized the rock was a lot bigger than it looked. It would make a huge splash if I could dig it out of the muddy earth.

After a few tries, I was able to get both hands underneath it. The rock was heavy and slimy. *Perfect.*

Just as I stood up, a flash of lightning danced across the pond in front of me. I didn't really know how lightning could just appear like that when there weren't any clouds around, and I felt funny for a second, kind of light-headed.

All of a sudden, I was down on one knee in the pond. My rock was back in the water in front of me. *How did that get there? Did I drop it?*

When I felt hot, gooey liquid running down my head and onto my shirt, I knew something wasn't quite right. James was standing over me and shouting, but I couldn't hear him, mostly because there was a loud ringing noise in my ears.

He kneeled in front of me and grabbed my shoulders. Finally, I could hear what he was saying: "You're bleeding!"

I hadn't seen lightning, but it had been a flash of light. When I stood up to throw my perfect rock into the pond, one of the neighbor's kids, who was standing behind me, had just thrown his. It wasn't very big, I was later told, so he was able to throw it fast enough to hit me right in the back of the head, hard enough to knock me down and cause a huge gash, which started bleeding, really bleeding.

I hadn't known before, but when a person gets hit in the head, there's a lot of blood up there that rushes out. Seeing my shirt turning all red made me stand up and try to run home, but my legs wouldn't work very well. I stumbled and fell into James, who was holding me up as we made our way through the woods.

"Take it easy, V. We'll be home in a sec."

One of the other boys had already run back to our house to get the grown-ups. A minute later, Dad was coming around the corner on the path to our house. He was running right at me, and in one quick movement, he picked me up in his arms then carried me home. At that point, I was totally out of it, and blood had soaked all the way through my shirt and down to my shorts.

In our driveway, Mom looked at me, and I heard her saying something about the hospital. But Dad was already loading me into the car. I was only starting to realize what was going on as Dad wove through traffic on the highway to the hospital. He drove really fast, and after we arrived, I was back in his arms again as he carried me into the emergency room.

I got eleven stitches in my head that night. It didn't hurt too much, but I remember being upset that they'd shaved part of my head for the stitches. The next morning, Dad came into my room with a new Red Sox hat for me to wear over my bald spot. He told me that I was very brave, and he sat with me as we relived what had happened at the pond.

As soon as he'd found out I'd been hit by that rock, Dad took control. Mom once said that while she might be the doctor in the house, she saw the Marine in Dad come out that night. He was in charge and wasn't going to let any more bad things happen to me.

I wore that Red Sox hat long after I got my stitches out and my hair grew back. It's too small for me now, but it hangs on a hook in my closet. I've been staring at it this afternoon, so I get up from my bed and take it off the hook.

Dad is coming home from the hospital today. I put my hat on the bedside table in his room to be there for him when he gets back. Maybe it still has healing powers.

* * *

I have to admit that I didn't really concentrate in remote class today. I told Ms. Doodle about Dad coming home, and she was so happy for me that she gave me a big loud air-hug through my iPad, yelling, "Aaair-hug!" at the top of her lungs in a silly voice.

The GirlZ are excited too. Katie called me after class and asked about how it was going to work with quarantine and taking care of Dad.

"What's it been like with your mom back?"

"Amazing," I say. "I don't miss having to visit her only on certain days of the week or whatever, and I really don't miss having to stay at her condo. It's nice, but it's not the same."

Katie looks down to the bottom of the screen for a second. "Do you think your parents will be okay… being together?"

I've been thinking about that quite a bit. How could I not? "Honestly, I don't really know, but I think so. Mom keeps saying she's only staying for a week or two, but it's not like there's a lot of choice at the moment either. She says that Dad needs to be in his room for a while, and she'll need to help him and help us. She said, 'It is what it is.'"

Katie says she has to go and gives me that big Katie smile while signing off. "Call me later if you can! Bye!"

I walk downstairs, and James is sitting on the porch, playing with Buster. "Hey, V."

"Hello, brother." I sit down next to him as Buster wanders off to pee in Mom's garden, leaving us alone, looking expectantly down the street. James is kind of quiet, which isn't totally unlike him lately.

After a moment, he looks over at me and exhales. "Phew."

"Right?" I say back.

James nods. "I was really scared about… I mean, I didn't know if he was coming back."

"I know, James. Me too." I lean into his shoulder for a moment. He doesn't flinch. We don't elbow each other. We just sit and wait, just like we have been doing all week long.

When Mom's car comes toward our house, we stand up at the same time, and I start waving and dancing. I run down the driveway. Mom and Dad have their masks on, and Dad is waving at me from the passenger seat as they pull into the driveway.

When he steps out of the car, I charge at him full speed but stop abruptly as a weird thought occurs to me. "Can I give you a hug?"

Dad looks at Mom, and they both smile as he says, "Of course, honey."

I wrap my arms around his waist, and Dad hugs me back for a long moment. Then he says, "I missed you guys," as James crashes into him too. "And I missed these hugs!"

Buster went back into the house, which seemed like a good idea at the time, but now he's going crazy, barking and jumping at the door. Dad is Buster's favorite, and for a second, it looks like Buster might charge through the screen door.

Mom must have the same thought, because she says, "James, you'd better let Buster out before he destroys the house."

James runs up the steps, opens the door, and practically gets knocked off the porch as Buster gallops right by him toward Dad, who is down on one knee, waiting. Buster runs him over, licking him and jumping all over the place. Dad is laughing, and so are we. Even Buster knows that it's a happy moment for all of us. Mom unloads Dad's things from the back seat, and all five of us walk into the house together, tails wagging.

"I'll put your things in the room, and you can get settled," Mom says to Dad at the door. "Want to sit on the porch for a bit? I'll get you a coat."

Dad nods as he turns toward his favorite chair and sits down, resting his elbows on his knees and looking at James and me.

"How are you feeling?" James asks from the chair across from Dad.

"I feel great to be home. To be out of the hospital. It wasn't a long time in the grand scheme of things, but it sure felt like it there for a while."

"Do you still cough a lot?" I ask.

Dad smiles from under his mask. "Just a little bit now, honey. Not as bad as before. I'm doing better."

Mom steps outside to join us, holding Dad's coat. "Warm enough?"

"Perfect."

We sit there and talk as Dad asks us questions about remote school and whatever else we did over the past week, until Mom tells us that it's time for Dad to get into bed.

He nods. "I think that's a good idea. I'll rest for a little bit, and we can talk more later."

Dad stands up slowly and looks at us. Then his gaze wanders over the front yard. He throws a ball to Buster, who sprints full speed until he catches up to it. Buster barrel-rolls forward as he snatches it up between his teeth.

As Dad turns to walk inside, he puts his hands on our shoulders to look at us for a long moment. "It's good to be home, kids. I missed you."

"We missed you, too, Dad," James and I say.

With our arms around each other, we walk into the house and up the stairs. I'm going to hold on to him tightly until I believe this is all real. Mom is doing something in the kitchen, so James and I lead Dad into his bedroom.

"We left you some books and brought in extra pillows," I say as we walk through the bedroom doorway.

"So I see. Thanks, Vivian. Oh... here's a little something I haven't seen in a while." Dad studies my old Red Sox hat that I left by his bedside table. "Is this for me?"

I smile. "I thought it might help you feel better."

"Yes," Dad says, smiling. "I think this hat has special healing powers, if I remember correctly?"

"Exactly." I close the door behind me. *Dad's home. He's going to be okay.*

Dad ends up sleeping throughout the afternoon and almost past dinner. I mostly leave him alone since Mom told me not to bug him. But one time—okay, two—I open the door just a bit to look in on him when no one is around, listening for sleeping sounds. *All good.*

James and I have remote school the next few days, which is totally fine with us. We're both excited to be home with Dad, and I'm always excited to live in my pajamas and make pancakes, especially with Mom next to me in the kitchen.

CHAPTER SEVENTEEN

THE LIGHTKEEPER

IT'S BEEN TWO WEEKS SINCE Dad got home, and I am all sorts of mixed up. Dad's doing great. He's able to be downstairs more than upstairs, cook meals, and take short walks with us and Buster to get his exercise. Mom has been with us while she works some days from home, doing telemedicine, but with Dad doing better, she's able to go back into her office more often.

The four of us are together for the time being. What's more, Mom and Dad talk to each other. They sometimes sit near each other in the family room or on the porch. There's conversation around the dinner table.

But I know what's coming. I don't like to think about it, but soon, Mom is going to move back to her condo. I've lived in a pretend universe where this doesn't end. In my fantasy, Mom and Dad stay here together, and we go back to the way things used to be when they were happy. When we were all happy. But as the days go on, I know this fantasy won't last, and it feels like an abrupt end to a glorious vacation is coming soon. I can tell that this is on their minds, too, creating a new kind of awkwardness around the house. It's different from when they were fighting, but a new anxious layer is hanging over us.

As I'm just about to crawl into the comfy warmth of my bed, my tablet dings, and there's Katie's smiling face. "Hi, V! How's it going over there?"

"We're good. Thanks for coming by with the flowers today."

Katie and Mrs. Adams knocked on our door this afternoon for a short visit with Dad and to give us some flowers. Now that we're out of quarantine, our friends are able to come by more often.

"Of course," she says. "My mom told me on the way home how happy she is to see your dad up on his feet. He really looks like he's getting better!"

This gets right to the heart of the thoughts nibbling around the edges of my brain. So I shake my head at Katie, as if doing so shakes some of these thoughts loose so they can fall out of my mouth.

"I've been thinking a lot about my mom and dad," I say as I take my iPad and Katie's face into the fort.

Katie's smile dims just a bit.

"When Dad first came home, Mom was checking in on him, bringing him meals in his room, and that meant they were spending time together. I always wondered what they would talk about. I'm sure a lot of it was about how he was feeling, but as the days went on, would they ever talk about them? About us?"

Katie nods, almost shrugging. "Well, that's good. At least they're talking."

"You're right, I guess," I say back, not so sure.

"Have you seen them fight?"

Katie has heard her share of stories about my parents, so it makes sense that she, of all the GirlZ, would ask that question.

"No. I mean, I guess I haven't thought about it that way. They haven't fought at all since Dad came home…"

This idea is now taking root in my brain, pushing out some of the previous uncertainties.

"Well, there you go," Katie says. "Even if they go back to being, um, not together again, at least maybe this time, being together leads to less fighting."

"I know, but I… I wish they would stay together…" My voice trails off when I finish the thought as it occurs to me this may never, ever happen.

Katie's smile is now gone. She's staring at me with more of a frown, which is seriously weird. I've seen this look on her face on the soccer field, especially when she has the ball and is about to shoot.

"Vivian, there's nothing you can do about that, and you need to stop pretending that you can." Katie says this so matter-of-factly that I'm speechless for a moment. There it is: stark reality, confirming what the voices in my mind have been saying but I resist listening to. I can only stare at her.

"I'm sorry," Katie adds. "I don't mean to be harsh, but can't you accept that at the very least, your dad is okay, and maybe your parents' new normal, even though they are still apart, will mean them being nicer to each other?" As the smile comes back to her face, Katie says, "These are good things."

The Lightkeeper and her magic superpowers are at work. I roll over onto my back and turn on the mini star projector. *The new normal. The better normal.* My family isn't the same, but in spite of everything, we're at least a little better. That new realization lifts me up, lightens me, and makes me feel hope for what's ahead.

The only problem is, I'm still speechless. What's my comeback to all that wisdom? *Jeez, Katie is like a grown-up sometimes—that's it!*

"You know what? You're like a grown-up!" I say, like it's an insult.

There it is—the ear-to-ear Katie smile is back. She cracks up and gets all dramatic like I'm mocking her. "Stop it. Am not!"

The laughter continues until Mom tells me to settle down. Katie yawns and says she's tired anyway, so we smile at each other and sign off.

Alone with my thoughts, I float in space in my fort. I've had a lot to think about these past few weeks. Maybe it's time to give my brain a rest and just go with it. Just like drifting off to sleep…

CHAPTER EIGHTEEN

SATURDAY

EITHER MY PARENTS DIDN'T CHECK in on me last night or they just decided to let me sleep in my fort, because that's exactly where I find myself the next morning. I had a heavy sleep. I know it because of all the drool falling off my cheek and onto my pillow. *Ick.*

I roll over and look at the time on my iPad. *Not too late yet. Still time to wake up slowly.*

Apparently, that's not the case in the Adams household, as I already have a text from Katie, sent early this morning: *I'm so psyched that you're playing this weekend. We need you back in goal! Soccer ball emoji. Strong arm emoji.*

I write back: *Me too! Can't wait! Heart emoji. Thumbs-up emoji.*

It's true. I'm so excited to get back on the soccer field again. I've missed my soccer sisters and the action of the game.

Katie texts back: *Do you want to ride bikes over to the game together? Bike emoji.*

The field is only a few minutes away from our neighborhood. I usually bike over to pick up Katie, and we ride to soccer practice together.

Me: *I think my dad wants to take me. He says he is feeling well enough to come watch from the sidelines for a little bit.*

Dad hasn't been coaching during his recovery, but he said last night that seeing us play this weekend will make him happy. He misses being around all of us kids.

That makes me wonder about the plan today. Some kids who have divorced parents never get to have their moms and dads at a game at the same time.

I hear a knock on my door, followed by Dad's "Good morning, honey."

"Hiii," I chirp from the fort.

Dad makes his old-man noise as he sits down and pulls the sheet back to look in on me. "Hi there. Want some breakfast?"

"Yep." I stretch across the length of the fort bed.

"We need to get you fed so we can get moving this morning. We have your game and James's game right after that."

"Dad, do you think Mom will watch the game too?"

Dad keeps that same smile, but it takes him a second to say, "Probably. I mean, I'm pretty sure."

I say, "Okay," but Dad is still looking at me.

"Does that worry you, Vivian—that Mom and I might not want to be at the field together?"

"I guess I just thought about it earlier. That's all."

Dad turns to look across my room, as if thinking about something. "Nothing makes your mom or me happier than watching you and James doing things, honey. Whatever we're going through, we won't let it get in the way of cheering you on at soccer. I know she would say the same thing if she was up here right now."

Dad kisses me on the forehead then rudely pulls the blankets off me. "Now, get your butt out of bed!"

"Aaagh!" I laughingly yell and kick at him.

Saturdays in the fall tend to bring a lot of activity to our house. I always have a soccer game, and James always has a baseball game. The only question is, are we home or away? Also, who's driving whom and where? Actually, I guess that's a lot of questions.

Today is the same thing. When I finally make my way downstairs, Mom is already making pancakes, and Dad has moved out to the porch to enjoy a cup of coffee while reading the paper.

"Hi, honey. Sleep well?"

"Hi, Mom." I yawn and stretch at the bottom of the stairs. "Can I have chocolate chips in my pancakes?"

"How about bananas or something healthier on game day?"

That makes no sense whatsoever. I just stand there looking at Mom without blinking.

"Okay, Vivian. Chocolate chips with banana slices too. That's the deal."

Victory. I smile and do a little twirl in my bathrobe.

James is in the family room, watching some sports show. *Snore.* So I try to steal the remote to watch something—anything—more fun than that. He reaches over to grab it back, so of course, I kick at him, making all my pretend-ninja sounds.

"Guys…"

"Sorry, Mom."

We settle on watching a soccer game going on in England, and I veg out on the couch, taking in the smell of the pancakes from the kitchen and the fresh fall air coming through the open window. The fragrances mix together throughout the house. Buster strolls over and nudges my foot with his nose before lying down next to me, looking for a belly scratch.

"Hey, Buster, buddy, buddy…"

I hear Dad come back in through the front door and look up to see Mom turn around from the stove.

"Want a warmer-upper?" Mom reaches for the coffee pot. She and Dad used to have their own language sometimes. I haven't heard it in a while, but *warmer-upper* is a phrase borrowed from Saturdays from a long time ago.

Dad smiles. "Thanks. The pancakes smell good."

"Mom's putting chocolate chips in mine!" I announce from my lazy position on the couch.

"Oops," Dad says. "Were those chocolate chips for you, V? I'm sorry. I ate them all before bed last night."

I roll my eyes at Dad because I know he's just trying to annoy me. "Ha, ha. You're sooo funny, Dad."

"Come on in for breakfast, guys. All set," Mom says.

"Anyone want to hear my twenty-page pregame speech?" Dad asks as he chews on his pancake. "I'm going to visit the bench today and have been practicing for the past two weeks. Something to motivate the girls before they take the field in all their soccer-girl glory."

"That sounds like a not-so-great idea," James says, rolling his eyes. "Are you coaching today?"

"No. Not today. I want to come watch from the sidelines so I can relax and enjoy myself. I'll be back behind the bench maybe next week, when I have a little more energy."

Mom nods and offers a little smile. "Oh, good. Someone has come to their senses and is not rushing their recovery." She sips her coffee and gives Dad a little look, which makes him smile as he digs into his next bite.

As it turns out, everyone is coming to watch my game today, even Mia and Lucy. That makes me happy, but the bummer part is that then I have to go watch James's baseball game in the afternoon. *Snore.*

* * *

All my soccer sisters are excited to see Dad, and the other coaches make a big dramatic introduction when he approaches the bench. As usual, Dad adds his own silly energy by saying some dorky, supposed-to-be motivational pregame speech. But the team loves it.

It feels great to be back on the field again. Katie is on fire today with a little extra something in her step every time she makes a run toward the other goal. Midway through the first half, Mel makes a perfect pass up the middle, releasing Katie on a breakaway. A defender tries to slide-tackle into Katie, but Katie jumps over her like she isn't even there and pushes the ball downfield at full speed. The goalie charges at her to try to take the ball, but no chance. Katie shoots the ball with her right foot so hard that the goalie freezes in place, watching it fly by. The ball clangs off the inside of the post and ricochets violently across the back side of the net before settling on the other side of the goal.

Katie turns and sprints back upfield with her arms spread wide like wings on an airplane. Mel and all of my teammates run alongside her past the midfield line then slide on their knees, pointing at me. Katie screams with a huge smile on her face and pigtails bouncing—an explosion of athleticism and joy, mixed with some serious girl power. I stand there with both arms in the air, screaming, "Yesssss!" right back at them.

The game ends as a big two-to-zero win for us and a shutout for me.

After the final whistle, Dad runs up to hug me and congratulate the other girls. He puts his arm around Katie. "Been practicing that shot much?"

"Yep! And the celebration slide too—just for you, Vivian!" She steps closer to me. "I love that you're our goalie. We all know that we can depend on you back there."

A bunch of us players sit together with our post-game ice cream while Mom takes James home to get ready for his game. The other girls run back onto the field and try to imitate Katie's celebration slide. It's not so easy while holding ice cream, leading to some funny—and messy— incidents that we girls find funnier than the parents do.

On the drive home with Dad, we relive the high points of the game. As usual, he can't stop talking like a coach, but that's okay. I had so much fun, and I'm still so energized that I could talk about it the whole ride home. So I do.

"It was a great game to watch, Vivian. I'm so proud of you."

I'm proud too. So much so that I don't even feel totally bothered about the thought of going to root for James at a baseball game. Fortunately, James is pitching today, at least making the game more interesting than usual. And I get to sit next to Mom, so we can talk the whole time.

Okay, fine. James pitches really well, and his team goes on to win an exciting game. I know I get fussy about sitting through his games, but I also know that James works hard at baseball, so I'm happy to see him have a good game.

"Nice job, brother."

"Thanks, sister." James is smiling, happy about the win. "It's been a good day."

It sure has. The day was filled with playing sports and thinking about nothing else. Throw in two exciting games, two wins, and ice cream—and everything else fades into the background. Except for the amazing feeling of enjoying it all as a family.

At least for today, everything feels really... nice, and we're all together. I still don't know how long it will last, but I remember what Katie said. *Normal.* It's the new normal, maybe, and it's pretty good.

CHAPTER NINETEEN

FOREVER SLEEPOVER

"SHHH! You guys, stop. We are going to get in trouble."

Of course, this makes everyone laugh even more. The fort is about to fall over again, and we'll have to rebuild it for, like, the hundredth time tonight. *Just need to make a few quiet repairs over here, a tuck over there. Perfect.* The bedsheet roof might hold this time.

"Flash the light over here, Katie."

Lucy whispers, "Vivian, your dad said to be quiet and go to sleep."

"I know, I know. I just need to tuck this sheet under these books to hold it in there… oops!"

Crash!

"Oh no! Mia, hold that chair up!"

Crash!

Everyone freezes for a second, trying to silence the unavoidable giggle fit. But predictably, it doesn't work.

A growl emerges from Dad's room. "Girls! Come on! It's past eleven! Either fix your fort or save it until tomorrow, and *go to sleep*!"

Uncontrollable, tear-inducing giggles turn into stomach-cramping laughter as we're lying on the floor, hands over mouths, eyes squinting and wet with laughing tears. Pillows, sleeping bags, flashlights, lanterns, and blankets mixed with structural-support material of chairs, books, and sheets are all now in a big, jumbled pile.

We lie on our backs, holding our stomachs and trying to quiet our laughter, which never works. So, more laughter. Then footsteps.

Uh-oh.

The door opens. Dad's here to shut it down. "Ladies… it's really late."

"Sorry, Dad." I giggle.

"Listen, I don't need you to go to sleep, which obviously you're not ready to do anyway, but can you leave the"—Dad looks around the room with a little smile, betraying his tired eyes—"fort, or whatever this mess is, until tomorrow? Just keep it down, or I'm coming back in like the Stay-Puft Marshmallow Man."

"What do you mean, Stay-Puft Marshmallow Man?" I ask from under my blanket.

More laughter.

"That's such a Dad thing to say!" I say from under my blanket.

"Shush it, girls!"

"Okay. Okay. Sorry. We'll be quiet."

Dad closes the door, leaving us to settle down, and we're able to breathe again just a little. Mia is still laughing, quietly at first, but then she snort-laughs loudly enough to wake the whole house when Lucy pokes her in the ribs. That's it—there's another whisper-laughing burst. Legs kick the air as we roll around, burying our laughter in blankets, bears, and puppies. Sleepovers are my favorite thing.

We can do sleepovers now. Vaccinations are finally everywhere. Our parents say now that they're vaccinated and that people like our grandparents are vaccinated, a sleepover is safe again. For a while there, I didn't think I would see the day.

Dad makes pancakes the next morning, layering on the syrup, butter, and Nutella, of course, along with chocolate chips. We GirlZ are all in our onesies, still warm under bathrobes.

"I don't think there's enough coffee in the house to wake me up today," Dad says as he flips the pancakes over in the skillet. Weekend smells of cooking, coffee, and heat on in the house drift through the air. This is home.

Dad goes on, "V, do you have your soccer stuff ready to go for today? Practice is at eleven."

"Mom said she left my stuff in the dryer."

"Mom isn't very happy with you girls right about now," Mom announces as she walks down the stairs into the kitchen, sneaking up behind me to tickle me in the ribs. "Hi, girls. Everyone 'sleep well' last night?"

"Huh? Oh, hi, Mom."

What the…? Mom spent the night. I thought she was going to leave last night after we all settled into my room.

Mom moved back to her condo not long after that special sports-filled Saturday we all had together, because Dad was finally feeling better and could handle things on his own. But before Mom moved out, she and Dad told us about their idea for a new plan. Instead of James and I going to visit Mom at her condo, she would come here to the house for dinners, like last night, or for an afternoon with us whenever she wants. No more scheduled visit days. No more sleeping in another bedroom at her condo that isn't really mine.

When I asked her about this new arrangement, Mom said that she likes her little visits here at the house. "It gives me and Dad time to talk about things and space to go think about things—about us." Grown-ups make everything so complicated.

Oh, I almost forgot. "Mom, are we still all going to Mia's house tonight?"

"I hope so," Mia says. "Mom's been cooking for, like, a week to get ready."

"Uh-huh," Lucy says through a big bite of pancake. "And my mom made her cheddar cornbread and is bringing the desserts."

"I'm thinking this was a poorly timed sleepover." Mom yawns before sipping coffee. "But yes, girls. Don't worry. We wouldn't miss the party of the year."

The GirlZ gather their piles of stuffed animals and other sleepover paraphernalia when the other moms arrive a short time after breakfast. We are psyched for tonight's big cookout at Mia's house. On the other hand, the moms are complaining about being *oh-sooo-tired* because of my mom dealing with our sleepover and Mia's mom having apparently cooked all week. *Blah, blah, blah.*

Mom pours herself another coffee then pours herself into the comfy chair in the family room. I follow and plant myself on her lap as she sips her coffee with one hand and strokes my hair with the other.

Dad walks in and smiles. "Well, this looks perfectly cozy." He and Mom look at each other for an extra-long second with goofy grins on their faces.

"What?" I ask.

Dad just smiles at me.

"What?" I ask again and spin around to look at Mom. She also has this weird expression—a smile, but one eyebrow goes up.

Mom looks at Dad and asks, "Want to get James in here?"

James has been holing up in his room all morning to avoid all the girl chaos taking place in the kitchen.

"I think that's a fabulous idea." Dad turns and asks James to come downstairs.

Something's up. I'm not sure what, but it feels like something of a family meeting is about to take place. We've all been spending time together during Mom's visits, but it's not like we've had something so formal sounding. Well, Dad did say "fabulous" at least, so it can't be bad news. I turn to look again at Mom, who winks at me with a little smile.

"What's going on?" I ask just as James walks in with Dad.

"What's up?" James asks.

"James, have a seat." Dad lowers himself onto the couch to face Mom and me. James and I just look at Mom and Dad expectantly.

Dad speaks first—more like fumbles along. "Guys, your mom and I have been talking a lot lately… about us. Um, all of us… together. About being together."

"Huh?" I ask. *What the…?*

"Oh, come on, Jim," Mom says. "Want me to say it?"

Dad is smiling and even looks like he's blushing a bit.

Mom leans forward and kind of turns me around in her lap.

"Why don't you two boys move over a bit?" She picks me up, making kind of a Dad noise, and we step across the room to sit next to James and Dad on the couch.

"Your dad and I have something to tell you guys—some good news. We want to tell you that I'm staying here. At home. With you—all of us."

Mom looks at Dad, who nods and says, "We're getting back together."

James's mouth drops open. I shriek, maybe even scream, like lightning just flew through me, toes to head. I stand straight up and whip around to face them, staring at Mom and Dad. They're holding hands now, looking at me and James, smiling widely.

"Well? What do you think about that?" Dad asks.

I jump into all three of them as James leans in from the side—a big pile of muffled laughs and hugs. I'm speechless, caught by surprise, joy, and disbelief. Mom pulls away, and I just shake my head at her.

"Your dad and I worked through some things these last few months. We realized that we weren't really happy being apart from each other, but at the time, we thought that was our only option."

Dad says, "But then Mom and I were sort of forced to be together when I got sick. There was nothing to fight about then but plenty of time to just talk. So we did. About a lot of things. We started to like being together again. Then, when Mom moved back to her condo, we changed the visit plan to try to see if we would still like being together, even if we didn't have to be now that I was all better. We found that being apart gave us space to, well... realize that we missed each other."

"That's right," Mom says.

"Lately, your mom and I have talked about what being together as a family means to us, and it's important for me to hear what it means for Mom and for her to hear it from me."

Dad points at the picture of him, Mom, and their friends from that day they met at the restaurant, which is now back in its rightful place in the family room, in plain view. The story of them.

"And you know what?" Dad asks. "I once met Mom, then I lost her, and then somehow years later, I met her again. I don't want to take a chance on the third time being a charm."

Mom smiles. "I'm very happy to say that we won't ever need to find out."

CHAPTER TWENTY

SUPERGLUE

MOM AND I DECIDE TO take Buster for a walk because James and Dad are hogging the couch, watching a boring baseball game. The late-afternoon sun is just beginning to dip, showing off leafy-tree shadows that lean into our yard in the evening. Buster is pulling on the leash, always excited to have Mom and me to himself. I think even he realizes that something amazing just happened. My parents' news still fills the house with a happy atmosphere that hasn't been here in years.

The pond trail is quiet, with the exception of those late-day bird noises I love so much. One happy dog walker stops for a visit with Buster, and all the usual dog sniffing makes Buster's tail wag.

As we continue our walk, Mom says out of nowhere, "I was thinking about whether or not you ever figured out your superpower. Remember that conversation?"

I do, and I say so, laughing a little bit.

"I've been thinking it might be resiliency, Vivian. That's what I see in you. You've been through a lot this year and came out okay. More than okay."

I nod, and we continue along the trail, holding hands, while I let the thought roll around in my brain. I know what Mom means, but I have some ideas of my own on the subject. My mind flashes back to that horrible night when I was alone in my bedroom, sobbing, as I felt so sad and low. All my emotions completely overwhelmed me, so much so that they literally drove me to the floor under what felt like a big rock of grief mixed with panic. I was so sad about my parents and my dad getting sick, and I was so fed up with this year in general, that I didn't know if I would ever be happy again.

The superpower thing is supposed to be kind of funny, like the power of *patience* on Mom's coffee mug. But it's more than that. Katies positivity, Lucy's quiet spirit, and Mia's protective instincts are all deserving of actual superpower status.

And as for me? Well, that night at Mia's house when she said that I was the glue that held all of us together, I realized that I held myself together this year too, and that's saying something. So, yes, I get the resiliency thing. But an entirely different word comes out of my mouth. "Superglue."

Mom stops walking. "Huh? You mean Super*girl*."

"No! Super*glue*," I say, laughing.

Mom looks totally confused, so I go on, "I know it's a funny sounding superpower, but when I was really sad,

I learned that I have the power to deal. I can hold myself together, like glue."

Mom smiles a bit and says, "Well, that's a pretty cool superpower when you say it like that."

"Mia was the one who made me think of it, but it's more than just about me."

"What do you mean?"

"It's kindness. Like, when I was there for Lucy when she was sad or when Katie threw a pop-up dance party on our lawn to pick me up. For Lucy, Mia, Katie, and me, kindness made us strong enough to get through anything, because we were never alone. We were always looking out for each other. That's the glue that held us all together, kind of like an unbeatable group superpower."

Mom is silent. She's standing in front of me with her back to the trail. Her arms are crossed, and that eyebrow is up. A huge smile arcs across her face as she says, "That's awesome."

But she hasn't moved yet. She's still standing there.

"What?" I ask.

She shakes her head, and I notice a tear in her eye, but she's still smiling when she leans in for a big, long hug. Buster wiggles between us to be included, which makes us both laugh a little, but Mom doesn't let go. We stand there in a warm hug, and that's when the reality of the news this morning hits me. This is us again. It's been hard on everyone for a long time, but we've made it. As Mom holds on to me, I'm pretty sure she's thinking the same thing.

THE END

ACKNOWLEDGEMENTS

One of the most consistent of consistencies if you read enough books, is that many authors thank their family members first and profusely on the acknowledgement page. There are no exceptions here. Writing can be as selfish as training for marathons or whatever endeavour requires long term commitment of solitary effort. But it is never truly solitary because it can't be. My wife and teen kids have been listening to me develop characters and ask questions of them for years. Their contributions are all over these pages.

And then there are the friends, the neighbors, the mom readers, the kid readers and the beta readers. There are even a few literary professionals out there who have helped a great deal. The amazing ladies at the Manuscript Academy for starters - not to mention their agency and publishing faculty who offer consultations, take the time to read drafts and make us writers better (CeCe!). Thank you to the editorial staff at Red Adept and to the team at Streetlight Graphics who crafted the cover and the interior of this book.

Finally, thank you, dear reader for getting to know Vivian and her friends, and for supporting indie authors who just love to tell stories. There will be more adventures coming soon!

ABOUT THE AUTHOR

Rick's love of reading began in his childhood years and transformed into a passion for writing books for middle grade and young adult readers. An Indie Author, Rick is a member of The Society of Children's Book Writers and Illustrators and the Manuscript Academy.

Rick lives just outside of Boston with his wife and two teen children for whom he embellishes the dorky dad role. *A Bit About Vivian* is his debut novel.